LAWMAN'S DILEMMA

LAWMAN'S DILEMMA

"A lawman answers a call to a lawless town,
makes it fit to live in,
and then moves on to one that ain't."

A Reuben Braddock Western

by
RAY BILDERBACK

To order additional copies of this book, contact:
Xlibris Corporation
1-888-795-4274
www.Xlibris.com
Orders@Xlibris.com
104081

This for Madilane,
for the help, the patience

CONTENTS

PART ONE

Jasper Chase

1

The cheap new hat shielded Jasper from the brightness of the sun, but it sat stiff on his narrow head, and the crease was wrong. He would find a better hat. The shirt they'd given him he shucked early in favor of a worn blue denim from a backyard clothesline. It fell slack from his thin shoulders. The issue pants and shoes would have to do; he needed his money for a horse.

The second morning out, he started walking at daylight. Near noon he saw a huge live oak on the side of a small ravine. A wild grape grew up through it. Sure signs of water. A Pomo Indian sat in its shade. Two horses were hobbled on the bit of green spot that the spring afforded. One was a showy pinto, the other a dapple gray that showed mustang breeding, and by his flat forehead and prominent eyes, he also showed the Spanish. Jasper vetoed the pinto. Best not have a horse that memorable.

The Indian waved him to the spring. Jasper drank deeply and filled his canteen. There they bargained for the gray, settled on a price.

That much had gone well. A good young horse, the Indian said, and he was right, but it was a puzzle. How the hell did a Pomo know a good horse from a bad? Jasper paid in coins and, while he did so, studied the man's boots. They were cracked across the top, and the man had a wide foot. The Pomo could keep his boots.

The horse was Indian broke and mountain tough. Its mousy-gray color could take the heat but not draw attention to itself. Jasper rode it on a scrap of blanket also from the Pomo. He'd keep his eye out for a saddle. No use ruining a good horse riding bareback.

He took two days getting acquainted with the horse. Near noon of the second day, they holed up in a cool ravine just off Bear River. Snowmelt high in the Sierras had put the river nearly out of its banks. It had roiled its way through miles of riverbed torn up by hydraulic miners and arrived at this point a gritty brown tumble.

In the ravine, the spring water was clear and sweet. Once he had the horse settled, he drank deeply and ate handfuls of peppery watercress. Next he built a small fire against a granite boulder. From his issue shirt, serving double duty now as a saddlebag, he extracted a tin of beans and from his pocket a small folding knife. He liked the heft of the knife, the feel of the bone handle. Buying it, oats for the horse, beans, and a small amount of jerky for himself had left him without cash but with a growing feeling of independence.

With the knife, he opened the beans and carefully set them near the fire to warm. The knife he cleaned in the sand and slid back into his pocket.

Before the beans could heat, a pair of cowhands rode up. "Yer sittin' on Goodacre land, mister. Best you move on." The sandy-haired speaker was the younger of the two. His thin freckled face was twisted into a frown. He sat on a good-looking dapple gray that had loco eyes. The second man sat cavalry straight on a bay mare with a white nose blaze. He said nothing.

Jasper carefully placed a stick on the fire. "I figgered this'd be public land," he said. "Right here on the river. We won't do it any harm."

"That just ain't the point. Yer off the river apiece and on Goodacre land. No question 'bout it. Just move on while you can."

Jasper deliberately placed another piece of wood on the fire and smiled up at the man. The man, riled at that, turned red in the face and bailed off the gray, pulling his Colt as he came. He pointed the revolver at Jasper's midsection while he kicked sand on the fire. "What's it gonna take to get ya to listen?"

The man wore narrow boots, the new hardly off them. Jasper backed out of range of the flying sand. "Just hold on," he said. "There's no reason we can't get along. Your ranch could probably use a good hand. Happens I'm lookin'." This was a prevarication on Jasper's part; he had a ranch to go back to, was heading there now. It was a fertile little spread with sweet grass and plentiful water. He'd kept a picture of it in his mind, a picture that sustained him all the months in Folsom. He wore it in his mind like a talisman, rubbed it around in there like another man might rub a rabbit's foot.

The younger man was speaking to him again. "Yer lookin'?" He snorted. "Yer paler than a shoe clerk. You've either been in Folsom or really are a shoe clerk." He was laughing now. Pleased with himself, he kicked over the can of beans.

Jasper's jaw tightened, and his hand stole toward his pocket, then stopped midway. *The young fool is provoking you. Be patient. Give him no excuse to do you harm.* But Jasper was angry. When he'd stopped the horse at this spot, it seemed like luck was favoring them. Here they had a good place to camp and relief from the plague of mosquitoes they'd encountered on the riverbank. Then came this man to turn things sour. He was like the screws that made life miserable inside. There were names for such men and ways to treat them. More than that, there was a commonly held belief that some men argued for their own death. Here, it seemed, was such man. Let him argue if he wished.

"You men can see I ain't armed." Jasper said this including the big man on the second horse.

The sandy-haired man spoke again. "Worse luck for you." He fired two shots into the sand near the Pomo horse. "Now git."

The horse ran off fifty yards and stopped. The big man on the bay was restless. He spoke now. "Come on, Wilkie. There's no need for that."

Jasper put the image of the home place in his mind, rubbed it lovingly. He'd play humble if that was what it took. Backing off, he retrieved the scrap of horse blanket and the ill-fitting hat, which had come off when he dodged the ashes. "I'll just move on over to the river. There'll be no sign of me in the morning."

It was still muggy on the river; the swarms of mosquitoes had been joined by a like quantity of tiny black gnats. Jasper chewed a piece of jerky and ate a handful of the horse's oats. His best course of action was to melt into the hills without attracting further notice, and he knew that, but the meanness dealt out by the puncher burned in his craw.

By the time the weak quarter moon had settled its pale gleam on the river, Jasper had moved on. When the first rays of morning sun filled the Goodacre bunkhouse, they found Wilkie. His boots were gone along with his hat and his prized navy Colt. Hardly noticeable was the small dark hole where his skull and neck were joined.

2

Four horses plodded single file toward Stockton's new jail. The lead horse, a red roan, carried a tall figure. Bone-tired from two weeks on the trail, he defiantly sat erect in the saddle. Next came two hunched and trail-diminished prisoners tied hands and legs to a pair of bays. The fourth man, on a patient white horse, was tied across the saddle. He had stiffened into a half circle and was attracting flies.

It was dry and hot for April, and the town showed it. False front or brick, horse or human or tree, a film of dust had settled over all. As the procession neared the jail, the pair of stray dogs that followed it lost interest and dropped heavily into the shade of a cottonwood tree.

The tall man was Reuben Braddock. He was met at the hitch rack by a young deputy with a large ring of keys at his belt and a black-handled Colt tied low to his right leg. Braddock swung stiffly from the saddle. He gave the younger man a cursory look and decided that a desk job was the cause of the soft look. "Sheriff Muldoon in?"

"No, sir, he ain't. He's up at the statehouse . . . Sacramento. They're working out a plan to shut down the Castro Gang, maybe go after Marrietta."

Reuben stepped aside to give the deputy a better look at his following and gave it a nod. "This is the Castro Gang."

The deputy stared, gave Reuben another, more careful look, and quickly regaining his composure, announced that he was Gene Macy, jail keep.

Reuben nodded. "I knew a Cap Macy. He your dad?"

"Yes, sir. He's retired." Macy took another look at the prisoners, the body on the last horse. "I thought the Castro Gang was larger."

"It was. The folks at Jenny Lind took one off my hands. Lock up this pair. See to it they get food and water, *pronto,* but be finicky careful. They might try to bolt. Can't afford to lose 'em . . . got 'em this far." And then, indicating the third prisoner with a dip of his shoulder, he said, "I don't like bringing them in like that."

Macy offered his opinion. "These two don't look much better."

Reuben gave him a tired look. "Difference is, if you do your job, these men will look good in the morning. And if they don't, you'll answer to me."

Macy paled, dropped back a step.

Reuben had been harsh and instantly regretted it. "Sorry, Macy. I'm about a full day past worn out. You take care of my prisoners, and I'll get this one to the undertaker and the horses to the livery. If you need me, I'll be at Ma Jackson's."

The jail's office was stuffy and dark. It was tended by an elderly clerk wearing a green eyeshade, his sleeves held up by garters. The young jail keep jiggled his keys to get the clerk's attention. "I locked up that deputy's prisoners. He said they were the Castro Gang. He said the folks at Jenny Lind jailed one for him and he had one for Boot Hill. But why'd he bring 'em all this way? The ones I put up look half dead."

"While you were out eating lunch, I got a telegram. He's been on the trail better'n a week . . . caught the Castro outfit robbing the little bank at Burlson. He left one dead in Burlson and took the others to San Andreas for safekeeping. When he got there, the lockup was chock-full of rustlers."

"That deputy caught the four hisself?"

"Himself. The way I count, it was five, and he ain't a deputy. That's Marshal Reuben Braddock."

"Braddock? Wasn't he in the shootout at the Carlson Bridge? Broke up the William's gang?"

"The same man." The clerk put down his pen and half turned in his chair. "I was there that day with the posse. We heard shooting and then quiet. We rode like the possessed toward it. More shootin' and then an awful quiet again. Just the sound of our horses on the road. When we got there, the creek was running red below the bridge. His blood. Their blood. The horse's. And Braddock was in the water, all shot to hell, but he'd managed to crawl out and was lying on the bank. They'd ambushed him, you see. He'd been scouting for us and was riding back to report. When his horse reached the middle of the bridge, they popped up from under it, caught him in a cross fire. They'd'uv had him dead sure, but they were brothers, you see, and had competed all their lives, and so they hurried wanting to hit him first. As it was, he took lead in the leg but hid down behind the horse when it fell. The horse soaked up the stream of lead they poured at him and died right off.

"They watched the stream turn red with blood and thought they had him. By and by they looked up over the edge of the bridge. Nothing moved, so they rose together to charge him. Be sure he was dead, you see. He shot one between the eyes, turned, and downed the other one. But he took lead again and, when he tried to stand up, lost his balance and went over the side.

"When we got there, one brother was lying on the bridge, the other was in the water. Braddock was still trying to crawl out of the creek, but it was all instinct. He was out cold." He paused for a breath, realized he'd been staring out the window, staring across the years. "I'd never seen blood like that."

If the keep was impressed, he tried not to show it. After some moments of silence, he managed to say, "That was a few years back. I expect he's slowed some."

"Slowed some? Suppose you ask the pair you've got in lockup."

"Well, still . . . you've seen it, ain't ya?"

"Seen it?"

"Burlson, San Andreas. The country he was workin' in. They're sittin' on the edge of the gawdawfullest desert you ever saw. I heard say that the jackrabbits there carry water bags."

"I'd say if you're a Reuben Braddock, you go where you're needed. And I'd also say you won't catch an outfit like that with a set of keys."

The clerk turned back to his work, the hint of a smile on his face.

Reuben stood on the steps leading up to Ma Jackson's porch. She was sitting in a wicker rocking chair in what shade her porch allowed. A stout woman with heavy laugh lines etched into a time-wrinkled face, she wore her soft gray hair tied back. Her gray ankle-length skirt was protected by a starched white apron. What she first saw was a trail-gaunt man, all bone and gristle, bull hide tough. A wrangler maybe or an out-of-work stage driver? She had a mind to turn him away, send him to the hotel. Her little boardinghouse just didn't need the riffraff. But he seemed more than that. There was an air of authority about him. She stood up and stepped closer to him

He smiled. "Ma, you still make a mean biscuit?"

She moved a little more to get the sun out of her eyes. "Bless my buttons. You had me going, Reuben. And look at you, you're worn down to a nub. Just come on in. We'll get you a tub going. I'll make that pan of biscuits while you clean up. We've got catching up to do."

After he'd tied into her beans, beefsteak, and biscuits, they sat over coffee.

She leaned a little closer, looking deep into his hazel eyes. "You running from something, Reuben?"

He told her about the two-week stint tracking down the Castro outfit, breaking up their attempt on the bank at Burlson. "Well, it's no wonder you looked like the cat had drug you in. Don't feel like you need to be polite and make it down to supper . . . Sleep, sleep is what you need."

Noon of the next day, while he was checking his prisoners, the clerk caught him in the hallway leading to the cells. "Got a pair of telegrams for you, Marshal."

3

Jasper and the Pomo horse worked their way west and north, out of the flat land of valley oaks and into a landscape cut by river canyons and dotted with stands of black oak and pine, laurel and manzanita. Except for green spots around the blackberry-crowded springs, a warm spell had turned the meadow grass a pale yellow and filled the air with the oily tang of tarweed and chaparral.

Folsom Prison and the Bear River safely behind him, Jasper had but two things on his mind: getting home and getting even with Sheriff Charlie Prescott at Whistling Springs. It was Prescott who'd put him behind the bars at Folsom, and it was Prescott who had to pay. But the way Jasper had it figured, there was no hurry now. He'd ride through town, let Prescott see him, and he'd maybe hang around the bank a bit. It would give old Charlie something to think about and would serve until a more permanent arrangement came to mind. A cat playing with a mouse, that'd be the way.

The little horse with its great appetite for travel was cutting down the miles. Jasper felt expansive, felt like he'd left the bad stuff behind. He'd be arriving at the ranch early enough in the year to help his brothers with spring chores. They'd work the calves, then hustle through the haying. He could divide his time between the ranch and Charlie Prescott, and in a month's time, they'd be ready to trail the herd into the mountains and set up camp in Bear Valley. Eddy Sams and his daughter, Juanita, would have their cows there. It would be a summer of trout and blackberry cobblers, of hard work and beautiful country. And maybe the dark-eyed Juanita. Thoughts like this had kept him going at Folsom and accounted for the warm feeling he had now as he got closer to home.

On the afternoon of the fourth day, with a brassy sun hanging hot and high over his left shoulder and baking its way through his thin shirt, he came to the corner fence of the family ranch. Here the fence was still good and tight, the last work he'd done on the place four years back. He followed the fence line to a gate, entered, and rode down a slope to where young willows hung over the creek.

There were two deep ravines on the place that held springs. They were small but dependable, the backbone of the ranch. The stream in this ravine fed the cabin, the vegetable garden, and a pair of cedar stock tanks. He dismounted in the willows, and while the horse drank, he tipped back his Stetson and bathed his face. Taking a handkerchief from his pants pocket, he wiped at the shiny boots.

Mounted again, he nudged the cayuse in the ribs, urging it up the trail toward the cabin. The stream that should have been running briskly had shriveled to little more than an ooze here, and the pasture he was riding through had gone over to star thistles. Back under the digger pines, patches of tarweed and poison oak that he had carefully kept grubbed out were reasserting themselves. Worse yet, far worse in his mind, there were no cattle in the pasture. Hadn't been all spring by the looks of it. His good, warm feeling was eroding away.

Following a hunch, he rode through to the timbered second ravine and up to the high meadow where they raised oat hay. There was no hay to cut and no cattle in the range beyond.

He returned to the first ravine, topped a ridge, and came in sight of the four Lombardy poplars that grew near the cabin and had served as landmark for the past half century. In another moment, the ranch buildings came into view. Jasper was home.

At the cabin, a gaunt orange dog advanced stiffly from the shade of the pole corral, barking and wagging his tail. "Buster? That you, Buster?" He dismounted, scratched the dog briefly behind the ears, avoiding the patches of mange. "You still remember old Jasper." He fished in his shirt pocket and brought out a scrap of jerky, which he gave the dog.

He settled the horse at the corral and, since there was no hay in the barn, rummaged into the makeshift saddlebag for the last of the oats.

The barking had brought his brother Carl from the cabin. Carl, tall and thin as a young willow, smiled weakly and held out his hand. Just then, Calvin slouched out of the cabin, pulling on a soiled shirt as he came. Without a word, Jasper brushed past the two and into the cabin. The kitchen reeked of old garbage; the table was piled high with dirty dishes and whiskey bottles. He burst back into the yard where they were standing.

"Where the hell is the cows?" He stared at them, the hostility in him growing. He waited in silence. Reacting to the menace in Jasper's voice, the orange dog slunk to the back of the cabin.

"There ain't no exact answer," Carl began. "We had a bit of bad luck. Near run out of water a coupla summers back . . . Lost some stock that way. Pasture is poor . . ." He risked a look at Jasper and trailed off without finishing.

"A bit of bad luck? I suppose that's why everything I see round here has gone to hell in a handbasket. There was more'n a hundred head of good cows when I left, a crop of yearlings in the lower meadow"—Jasper was warming to his task—"wood in the shed, hay in the barn. And Buster . . . You said you'd goddamn certain take care of Buster."

He stopped, caught his breath. "If you'd kept the spring clean, you'd have water for the cows and a garden. If you'd planted oats in the high field, you'd have hay . . . But you didn't and you don't. So, what the hell have you been doin'?"

There was silence again with Carl toeing at the dust with his work shoe. "I'll tell you what you been doin'.

You've been drinkin' and gamblin'. Sold the stock off bit by bit . . ." His words carried a deep edge of sorrow.

If Jasper thought to get an answer, he was disappointed. Keeping the sun to his back and forcing them to look into it, he let the silence stretch out, the heat beat down on them. He kept them that way for the count of a hundred, then added, "Pissed it all away, didn't you? And I'm not hearin' you say you didn't. I'm hearin' you arguin' strong for what you got comin'. I'll be sleepin' in the barn till the cabin's clean."

4

Reuben Braddock pulled the bay's cinch strap tight and checked the pack on the roan he trailed. Just ahead of him was the little mining town of Whistling Springs. Three days back, while he was catching his breath at Ma Jackson's place, two telegrams caught up with him. One offered a job in Elder Creek, Nevada, and the other stated flatly that there was "trouble in Whistling Springs." Only that and nothing more.

The plea for help was from Maxine, the wife of his old friend and mentor, Charlie Prescott, sheriff of Whistling Springs. Maxine was not a woman taken to jumping at shadows. If she said there was trouble, you could bet on it. As to Charlie, he was stubborn as any two mules when backed into a corner and might be too proud to ask for help. But Maxine wasn't. So without asking who or what, Reuben turned his badge over to the clerk in Stockton and headed north for Whistling Springs.

Reuben drifted into the Springs trail dusted and wearing jeans stuffed into black working boots and a faded red shirt topped by a cow skin vest. With his black Stetson set low on his forehead and his shoulders drooping, he looked half asleep.

Whistling Springs boasted two blocks of weathered false fronts nestled on the west bank of the Yuba River. Reuben pointed the bay toward the squat building that housed Prescott's office. Years back, Reuben had worked as deputy for Charlie during the troubles at the Tule Flats diggings. He'd cut his teeth working for Charlie, and if you asked, he'd say there were two standout men in his life: his father, whose iron will had kept Elder Creek, Nevada, in order for twenty years, and Charlie Prescott. Their firm but fair-minded approach to keeping the peace had become his own.

From the shade of his Stetson, he studied Charlie's town. A block ahead, a woman and a child peered into the window of Widom's Mercantile. Just to Reuben's side of the mercantile, a man wearing a leather apron hurried into the bank. Two streets back, a thread of smoke rose from a garden rubbish pile. To his right and two doors past the sheriff's office, a lone horse switched flies at the hitch rack in front of a saloon. There were no buggies or farm wagons. The town was on the dead side of normal. Quiet. Too quiet. It looked like a town under quarantine.

Just then, a dusty rider entered the side street between Widom's Mercantile and the bank. Slender and square-shouldered, the rider stopped his small gray horse in the shade of two scraggly elm trees and dismounted Indian-style. With his hat pulled down and his collar up, there wasn't much of the man's face for Reuben to see. But the woman at the mercantile window recognized him. She grabbed her child by the hand and hurried up the boardwalk the way they'd come. Hair rose on the back of Reuben's neck. It was like he'd heard a rattler but was unsure of its location.

Keeping the bay at the same slow pace, Reuben continued on past the rider until Main Street took a turn toward the river. Once out of sight of the rider, he turned the horses down the alley and hurried to the back door of Prescott's office.

Sheriff Charlie Prescott was marooned at his desk studying a clutch of Wanted posters. But for a wisp of white hair above his ears, he was bald now. His thin hooked nose was set below a pair of steely gray eyes. A jiggling of the lock on his back door caught his attention, but before he could get to his feet, the door slipped quietly open flooding the room with sunlight. He slid back his chair and brought a navy Colt to bear on the open space. *No one there. Maybe the wind? No, damn it, I've locked that door.*

"Charlie?" The voice came from the alley. "You in there, Charlie?

He knew that voice. "Reuben Braddock!" He struggled out of his chair and holstered his revolver. "I guess you know, you scared the crap out of me." Reuben came in, blocking the outside light. "And damned if you haven't grown some. Now you take up a whole doorway."

Reuben reached out for a handshake. Charlie's hand all but disappeared in his grip. "I expect I have grown, Charlie. I wasn't much more than a kid when you took me in, showed me the business."

"Which I was glad to do. It's kept you in work, and word has it, you're goin' marshaling ag'in. Nevada this time. You come from there when you signed with me. Right?"

Reuben managed a grin. "I got an offer from Elder Creek. Haven't answered yet, but I'd be going home, Charlie. Ten years on one trail or another and not much to show for it."

"I wouldn't say that. You're already a legend, Reuben."

The grin left Reuben's face. "I'm famous for the wrong reasons. Last thing I want to be known for is the notches on my gun or a few pages in a dime novel. When I get to Elder Creek, I hope to settle. My father used to say, 'A good lawman tames a town, makes it worth livin' in, and then moves on to one that isn't.' I won't settle for that. There's not much sense in it."

"It's not likely to be that way, Reuben. You're known as an honest lawman, a fast gun with a conscience. Not many can say that. As far as settlin' down, it'll happen. Happened to me, happened to your dad."

"Guess that's so. You and Maxine been married thirty years?"

"Twenty-eight, Reuben, and soon as that lady hears that you're in town, she'll be expectin' a visit from you. Six o'clock is suppertime."

Invitation accepted, Reuben moved to where he could see the street but still be in the shadows. Charlie returned to the Wanted posters on his desk.

The quiet stretched out. Prescott looked up to see Reuben still at the door. "You see somethin' out there you don't like?"

"Oh, I don't know. Just habit, I guess. I'm watching a rider who is hanging out under the elms by the mercantile and, as it turns out, across the street from the bank. It's like he's waitin' for something."

Charlie tried to show a lack of concern. "Ain't no crime seeking a shade tree. Gets warm here even in the spring."

Reuben's gaze took in the opposite side of the street and his side all the way to the Mountain View and the livery stable beyond it. The rider by the elms was the only person in sight.

"Charlie, you got any posters there on the Chase brothers?"

"Nothin' new and just Jasper in the old posters. I'd guess he's out of Folsom now."

"As I remember it, he's got two brothers, Carl and Calvin. You seen them around?" Reuben asked.

"No, I haven't. They work a worn-out cattle spread in the foothills near Rough and Ready. I've heard it's mostly thistles and rattlesnakes. They don't come to the Springs since Jasper was put away."

"That Jasper, is he tall, thin, square-shouldered, walks with a little lurch? Keeps his hair long?"

Charlie had been on edge for days. His uneasiness came from the daily presence of the rider under the elms. Up to this point, he had managed to avoid admitting the obvious: it was Jasper Chase over there, and he didn't need Reuben reminding him of it. He snapped back, "Yeh. That sounds like him."

Reuben ignored the petulance in Charlie's voice and said, "Down Auburn way, all they wanted to talk about was a bunkhouse murder two weeks back. The man wanted for questioning fits your man across the street, horse and all." When he got no response from Prescott, Reuben persisted. "A man was murdered, Charlie. A bunkhouse full of men and one of them is murdered while the others sleep. They go on sleeping while his boots, his hat, and pistol are lifted. Don't that give ya the creeps?"

Charlie reached in his desk and pulled out a worn copy of a newspaper. "There's hell to pay, Reuben. No question about it. The *Journal* gives a full account. The murdered man is the son of Morgan Goodacre, who controls half the grazing around there. They've got a posse out turnin' over every rock."

"Wouldn't Chase come through Auburn if he just got out of Folsom?"

"He could have. But he could just as well have come a coupla other ways." Then Charlie surprised himself. It was like he was asking for help. "Why don't you stick around a bit? Tomorrow afternoon will be payday at the mine and the sawmill. The mine pays every week, the sawmill every two weeks, so tomorrow is a big day at the bank. Folks'll be doing business in town, and when evening comes, the hotel and the saloons will likely be jumpin'. Right now, I think you're workin' too hard."

An easy silence settled in. Reuben joined Charlie, and they pored over Wanted posters with Reuben returning every little bit to check Main Street. Suddenly, from the doorway, Reuben turned and faced Prescott. "That is Jasper Chase over there. Isn't it? You've known it the whole time."

For a time, Charlie didn't answer. He stared unseeing at the posters before him. At length with a heavy sigh, he gave in. "All right! You being so all fired interested, I'll tell ya. Four years back, I arrested Jasper for murder, but the court settled for a lesser charge. Now he's back, and he shows up here every day. Has for the most of two weeks. Seems like more."

"That so? Then the payroll ain't the answer. If he was after the payroll, he wouldn't be so obvious about it. Nope, there's something else he's after. I'd say he's grudgin' you, Charlie."

"Grudgin'?"

"Yep. Every day you've got to go through the gut-shaking worry over a bank robbery. But it doesn't happen. You just get your stomach settled down, and the next day he's back. This goes on day after day, and all that time, you got nothing to charge him with. Am I right?"

"That's about it. I can't charge him for sittin' under a shade tree, but I'd like to. He's got most of the town afraid of shadows. Some think we'd be better off if he'd just rob the damn bank and get it over with."

"I suppose you telegraphed Auburn. Told them he's here."

"Seems they're no longer interested and have jailed somebody else. If so, Jasper is off the hook."

"Could be they've got the wrong man, Charlie. How do you see it?"

"Could be Jasper done it, but we'll play hell getting proof of that in time to save that other man's skin."

"We can try, Charlie."

Reuben returned to the doorway. "Well, he's gone. Nothin' there now but the elm trees. Doesn't stay long, does he?"

"Like hell!" Charlie exploded. "Most days he's there for hours. There or at the saloon." There was a pause, then Charlie wondered, "Do you suppose you being here drove him off? He must have recognized you."

5

Jasper hadn't recognized Reuben. In fact, he couldn't remember seeing him before, but he smelled lawman. Leaving the spot near the bank, Jasper climbed to a high point near town, sat in the scrub oak, and waited. Two hours later, he allowed himself a small smile as he watched the big man check his horses into the livery and himself into the Magnolia hotel. Convinced now that the man was law and sure that he was staying in town, Jasper reasoned that the local law had been made doubly strong.

Two weeks sitting under the elm trees in Whistling Springs had given Jasper a measure of satisfaction, and he knew it was tormenting Charlie Prescott, but it didn't seem enough somehow. He yearned to do more. As he rode back to the ranch, he worked on a plan that would turn the beefed-up law enforcement to his advantage. It was a plan that could settle Charlie's hash for good and might teach Carl and Calvin a lesson as well. It wasn't a plan hatched by a healthy mind, but it suited Jasper.

Back at the home place, he found Carl sweeping the porch that ran the length of the house on the west side. "You and Calvin get the cabin clean?"

Carl shook his head.

"Get Calvin out here."

6

N oon the next day, Reuben watched from the office as Charlie left the bank and crossed the rutted street. "Things look good over there, Reuben. They're putting together payroll bags. Tension is a little high, but they've even got the bank president, Gabe Cassel, standing by with a double-barreled shotgun. There's been no sign of Chase." He rummaged around in his desk and came up with a badge. "Just the same, see'ins you're here, I'd like you to wear a badge."

Charlie stood at the door while Reuben tied on the badge. Business at the bank was picking up, customers coming and going. "Smooth as butter," he said and started back to his desk. "Like I said, I just wish he'd rob the damn place an' get it over with."

Two o'clock came and went. Reuben was restless. "When'd you say they'd come for their payrolls?"

"The mine will be there any time now. The mill picks up their pay sack a bit later."

An alarmed Reuben turned to him. "You might want to see this, Charlie." Jasper had ridden in from the west and was back at the elms. Two riders were coming up the street from the south. "If those are Jasper's brothers, I'd say you're getting your wish."

Charlie hurried to the door, looking around Reuben. The riders slid to a halt in front of the bank's hitch rack. Leading his own horse, Jasper hurried across the street to hold their reins. The riders pulled kerchiefs over their mouths. On seeing the lookout come forward, all doubt left Charlie's mind. "Damned if you ain't right. Out the back, Reuben. We'll ride straight into them and stop the whole thing before somebody gets hurt."

Seconds later, they burst out of the alley with Charlie riding on Reuben's left and slightly in the lead. Charlie rode straight at Jasper Chase and the horses he was holding. This forced Reuben wide of him and out of position.

At the sound of hooves, Jasper whirled around and fired twice without bothering to aim and dove in among the milling horses. Once there, he managed to heave himself onto his mustang. Hanging precariously to the offside of the horse, he was soon out of firing range.

Jasper had bailed out on his brothers.

Charlie yelled into the bank, "You men come out with your hands in the air. Give it up boys, we've got you covered."

Carl Chase was first out of the bank, a payroll sack clamped under his left arm. He fired two shots that went wide of Charlie. Thin as a snake, he made a poor target, but Prescott's second shot sent him sprawling in the dirt of the street. Carl gathered himself together enough to fire again. This shot caught both Charlie and the horse. They went down together in the dust of the street. Charlie fired as he fell, hitting Carl in his shooting arm. The fight was out for Carl. Charlie was pinned under his thrashing horse.

Twice a shotgun boomed from inside the bank, and Calvin, bent over and bleeding from the blast, came barreling out. He saw that Jasper and the getaway horses were far down the street, saw his brother Carl collapsed in the street, and tried to dive back into the bank, his pistol muzzle searching for Prescott as he fell. Reuben drew cleanly and deadly. His first shot caught Calvin in the throat. The next, a split second later, hit an already-dead Calvin in the chest.

A smudge of blue smoke hung over the scene. Before it cleared, Reuben swung out of his saddle and hurried to pull Charlie from under his thrashing horse. Unable to get past its churning hooves, Reuben stilled the horse with a shot to the head.

Men came running from all quarters and helped move the dead horse off Charlie. With two men down and needing care, Reuben sent for the doctor and gave up any thought of immediate pursuit of Jasper.

7

Reuben knew he'd get criticized by a bunch of armchair generals for not organizing a posse and chasing after Jasper Chase. But he figured that with just a little help from Carl, he'd find Jasper sooner this way. To his credit, he was more concerned with the care of the survivors than the care of his reputation. Accordingly, after helping Maxine get Charlie settled, he mounted the stairs to Doc Schmelling's little hospital, which amounted to a large room with two beds behind his second-floor office.

The doc was a tiny man, slight and hunched. Hanging over his face was a shock of gray hair that he kept brushing aside. He was standing behind a counter grinding powders when Reuben entered requesting to see the prisoner.

"Prisoner? He's my patient as long as he's here, Deputy. I've hardly got him settled and here you come." Instead of barking back at the doc, Reuben waited him out. This seemed to mollify Schmelling. "Well, you probably need to talk to him. He's a bit banged up but not much in danger. Still there's this: if he starts coughing, we'll have to call it off. Agreed?"

"Sure, Doc."

Carl was propped up in a cot by a window. His right arm was splinted and his rib cage swathed in bandages. He was a little weak but more than willing to talk. He told Reuben that he and Calvin had not wanted to rob anything but Jasper kept at them. It was their fault, Jasper said, that the home place had gone to hell, and they were damn sure going to set things right. Carl felt betrayed. "At the bank, he just up and left us. He was mad about the gambling . . . cows all gone, and Buster . . . Mostly it was about Buster. We'd let the mange get bad, and that was wrong, ya gotta say, but I had no idee he'd leave us like he did." He rolled toward the window and looked out at the river. More than a tiredness, there was a note of defeat in his voice when he resumed. "Left us to die." Another pause. "He said the bank'd be easy 'cause the deputy had quit. Said there'd be just old Charlie to keep off our back and he'd do that. But in the bank, they was expectin' us, and when we come outta the bank, the two of you was right there all hell on wheels, and Jasper had took off with the horses. Never meant to help us. We never had a chance." He turned back toward Reuben and the doctor. He looked puzzled. "It just don't figure. He wasn't never afraid of anything."

"Buster is . . ."

"Jasper's dog. Always was." Carl started coughing again. He seemed weaker. Doc Schmelling called an end to the session.

"Just one more question. Where did you and Calvin gamble?"

"Calvin, mostly. Grass Valley." More coughing. Carl turned onto his good side and curled up.

"That's all, Deputy." The little doctor showed Reuben to the door. Reuben was disappointed. He'd seen a dozen places in Grass Valley where a man could gamble, and likely, there were many more. He was about to make that point, but Schmelling shut him off with a head shake. "Try tomorrow."

Reuben pounded down the stairs to street level and struck out for Charlie's house. There'd be no waiting for tomorrow. Jasper's past was littered with the dead and wounded, and the trail was getting cold as a December wedding. It was obvious that someone had to stop Jasper, and it wasn't hard for Reuben to see that the job had fallen to him.

8

Maxine's yard was surrounded by a white picket fence. Hollyhocks were just coming into bloom, and the side yard was filled with the scent from a pair of apricot trees. A small white house with blue shutters sat deep in the lot. It had a settled, homey look that encouraged thoughts that Reuben had been pushing to the back of his mind.

Maxine joined him on the front walk. A slender woman, she had a calm and grace about her that he'd always admired. Her voice pitched low, she said, "Charlie is sleeping. He's got bruises on top of bruises, and the leg wound is serious. He bled so. I appreciate the care you gave him just after he was wounded. I suppose that bystanders, barflies, and a handful of others are going to be after you for not gathering a posse on the spot and charging off after Jasper, but it's likely that your staying with Charlie saved his life. That Chase boy's too." She paused for a moment, a wistful, motherly look on her face. "I wonder what made him do such a thing?" When

Reuben offered no comment, she went on, "I've got to say, I feel better having you in town and Jasper gone."

Maxine led him down the side of the house toward her kitchen door. Sunshine broke through a cloud, flooding Maxine's garden with light. Reuben stopped and breathed in the scent from the apricot trees. The humming of honeybees competed with frog racket in the cattail swamp next to the river. His attention wandered from there to the long green course of the Yuba River and the snowcaps on the far-off Sierras.

Maxine caught his mood. "You wonder, don't you, Reuben, how there could be such beauty and in that same world a man like Jasper Chase, a man who murders people in their sleep, turns on his brothers."

"Things get turned sideways sometimes and a man stops thinking straight. Like I started to say, Maxine. We haven't seen the last of Jasper." He hesitated, not sure just how to phrase it. "And . . . I'll stay on until he's . . . until that's settled."

"From what Charlie said, I gathered that you were anxious to move on . . ."

"Yes, I'll be taking the Elder Creek job. I just sent those folks a telegram agreeing to take the job, and though they're wishing me to hurry, I owe Charlie some of my time. More than that, likely." He looked at Maxine, a plea in his hazel eyes. "I let him down out there. It's a wonder he lived through it."

This declaration startled Maxine. "Why, you did nothing of the sort."

"I was slow, Maxine."

"That is not the way Charlie remembers it. Seems in his excitement, he got between you and the action. Got in your way." Reuben started to mount a protest. She put a finger to her lips. "Now, stop that. You're a mite quick blaming yourself. Let's just leave things the way he remembers them."

In the kitchen, Maxine consulted the clock on her china closet. "We can go in now. I've got to wake Charlie and give him his medicine. You can have a short visit. He'll never admit it, but we came awful close to losing him."

Charlie was propped up in a big wicker chair with a view out the bay window. A cup of broth gone cold was on the little table beside him. He roused at their entry, but his voice was weak and raspy. "Evening, Reuben, I must have dozed off."

"That's likely, Charlie. How's that leg?"

"Damn thing hurts in waves. Nearly puts me out, but these pills'll help. Other'n that, I'm weak as a kitten, but it ain't all bad. Doc says I gotta spend three, four weeks at home. Maxine says it'll be a second honeymoon. That's all pretty well settled, but it may be a while before I forgive you for shootin' my horse." He pretended to be angry, and one look at Reuben's sad face told him it worked. A small, tentative chuckle sent pain coursing through his damaged rib cage.

Maxine shot him a look. "Mark my words, your foolishness is going to be the end of you, Charlie Prescott. Reuben's here on business, and you're trying to be funny."

"I'm as sorry about that horse as you are, Charlie. Seems I had no choice." Reuben changed the subject. "I've been over talking to Carl Chase. In a month or so, he'll be able to walk into a courtroom, face the judge. Right now, he's confused and disappointed. Says that he and Calvin were never mixed up in anything like this before. They've never robbed anybody, never wanted to. Carl is a little simple maybe but straightforward. Says they went to Grass Valley for mange medicine and got in a poker game. Lost a bit of money, went back, and lost more. Wasn't long until Calvin had the bug bad. You know how it goes. Well, pretty soon they got in such a hole they had to sell cattle, then they went to gambling again to make the money back. It seems they couldn't remember what got them in the mess in the first place. Gamble, lose again. Gamble, lose again. Just a spiral."

Maxine lit a pair of lamps chasing the gloom from the parlor. Reuben continued, "I'm set on tracking down Jasper. My plan is to watch your house until first light then go looking for Jasper. If he isn't at the ranch, I'm going to believe he's headed to Grass Valley to get even with the gamblers."

"Doesn't explain to me why they tried the bank."

"Jasper bullied them into it. He made them feel guilty over the loss of the cattle. You saw how he'd sit across the street just to bedevil you. He did the same sort of thing to them. Day after day, kept after them."

"But he left them dangling."

"Could be it was his way of punishing them for wrecking the home place."

"He'd do that to his brothers?"

Maxine spoke up, "It doesn't surprise me, Charlie. It wouldn't be the first time we had a madman on our hands." She spoke with conviction but was shaken by her own observation. "And if that's true, he'll be back after you, Charlie. And you, Reuben. Carl. Most any of us. We've got to brace for it. That being the case, there are a couple of things you can do, Reuben, to help me get ready."

9

Jasper rode away from the bank job without a look back. When he reached the corner of his lower pasture, he tied the gray in the shade of the willows. Near the second post to the north of the fence corner, he dug up a cache of coins he'd hidden four years back. The canvas bag came apart when he tried to lift it, but the coins were there. They warmed the afternoon with their dull glow and brought a brief smile to his weathered face. He tied a pair of double eagles into the corner of his bandana and stuffed it into the left pocket of his jeans and put a trio of the golden eagles into his watch pocket. The rest he dropped back into the hole. The hole filled to his satisfaction, he struck out for the cabin.

At the cabin, he was greeted by Buster. He searched around inside his saddlebags and came up with a piece of jerky, which he shared with the dog.

Holding the saddlebags upside down and shaking them, he said, "You see here, Buster. We got no grub for us, no grub for the horse. Suppose we just ride to Grass

Valley, get some vittles and something for that mange. Call on ole Wah Gung. Could be he's behind this whole mess."

The orange dog riding behind the saddle, Jasper urged the little gray up the trail.

It was early evening when Jasper rode into Grass Valley. Parlor lights were beginning to show here and there, and saloon pianos were setting up a cheap racket. Careful inquiry at the Pastime Saloon told him he'd ridden right by Wah Gung's herb shop.

He retraced his steps. At the town's outskirts, he found the dozen shacks that made up the Chinese community. Wah Gung's place was three doors back in an alley that ended in a new stone wall that featured a round window. Behind the wall was a small formal garden. The shop was fronted by a dozen feet of new boardwalk and a sign in Chinese and English announcing it to be "Wah Gung. Herbs. Potions." The shop was showing signs of prosperity, and Jasper figured he knew why.

Jasper pushed open the shop door. From behind a silk curtain depicting a bamboo forest and a distant temple came the click of poker chips. He pushed aside the curtain. A young clean-shaven Chinese man in a silk jacket sat in the dealer's chair. He waved Jasper to a chair. "It's five-card draw. Table stakes with a three-dollar buy-in and a ten-cent ante. Jacks to open."

Jasper sat.

10

Next morning, the sky was cloudless with enough heat building to get Reuben out of his sheep skin vest. He folded it carefully and tied it behind the saddle. He was following Jasper's day-old trail past small farms hacked out of the red clay. He stopped at a patch of corn just below the road. A slender young woman looked up and brushed her hair away from a pair of tired blue eyes. She was nursing a trickle of water in an effort to keep the patch alive. "The Chase ranch? Yes, Depaty, the house is uht the head uh this draw. They got that whole hillside and up over the top and goodness knows how much more. There'll be a cross fence and a C-C burned inta the gatepost."

He found the gatepost all right and farther up the draw, flanked by a stand of Lombardy poplars, the cabin and its outbuildings. He sat off and watched the place for activity and, seeing none, finally rode in. There was no one there, not even the mange-ridden dog Carl talked about.

Poking about in the barn, he found the dog's bed, a round depression in the straw at the end of the barn nearest the cabin. In it were curls of orange hair. Nearby was another depression where a larger animal had been sleeping. On a nearby shelf, he found an empty cobwebbed bottle that had once held herbs for treating mange. Judging by a dust-clear ring, there had recently been another same-size bottle sitting neighbor to it. Brushing off the label with his sleeve, he read "Wah Gung. Herbs. Potions. Grass Valley." He added the bottle to his gear on the packhorse. Carl had said Grass Valley, and the bottle said Wah Gung. It gave him a place to start and took some of the guess work out of the pursuit.

The soft clang of a cracked bell was calling the faithful to meeting as Reuben entered Rough and Ready, and by early afternoon, he'd reached the bony ridge that marked the western edge of Grass Valley. Backed by pines, the Chinese cemetery was above the road on his left. A shallow freshly dug grave caught his eye. Every few paces leading up the hill to the cemetery, a punk stick sent up a greasy smudge along the roadside.

A swell of noise rose up the slope from town. He pulled the horses off the road, dismounted, and slid his rifle from the scabbard. In a few moments, around a clump of small pines scurried a procession of Chinese men. With an assortment of drums, horns, cymbals, and tin pots, they were making a terrible din. Trailing the makeshift band, a pair of men pushed and pulled at a handcart upon which precariously perched was a freshly built wooden coffin. Last in the procession, a small man sprinkled the roadway with paper flowers.

It was a Chinese funeral, and the flowers were a ruse; they were punched full of holes through which the newly departed carefully wound his way to thwart the devil, a devil who also had to carefully weave his way through all the holes.

The punk sticks and the noise were further efforts to ward off the evil spirit. Someone of consequence was getting a full Chinese funeral.

Reuben continued on. Just around the bend was a livery stable. A small sign declared it to be the Styx Stables, Ed Fipps Proprietor.

Reuben dismounted at the stable door and stood inside the shade edge briefly to let his eyes adjust. A large round-faced man was spreading fresh straw in the stalls. He ceased his labors and looked up at Reuben. "Get caught in the parade?"

"Yeh. Some notable man?"

"Wah Gung."

"Wah Gung, the herbalist?"

Ed Fipps set his pitchfork aside and came forward laughing. "He was that, and his sign says so, but Wah Gung was noted for his friendly poker game."

"Friendly?"

"Yes, friendly. I've played in 'em, and I've always won some hands and heard some witty stories, but I just never went away a winner."

"So, Wah Gung cheated."

"Wouldn't say that. Suppose we went in to play him. All we'd win from Wah Gung would be his ante. I'd win a hand, but it'd have your money in it. You'd win a hand, but it'd be my money. When Wah Gung stayed in, he'd win our money. Almost always, if he was patient, which he was, he came out the winner. Simple as that."

"Did he play for big money?"

"Big? You might lose a few dollars. No more than that."

"What about a herd of cattle, a ranch? Could you lose that in his game?"

"Not at Wah Gung's. The big games are downtown." A glint of sun on Reuben's badge caught the hostler's eye. "You here on business, Deputy? I'll help if I can."

Reuben reached a hand out to the hostler. "Reuben Braddock, and you must be Ed Fipps."

Fipps nodded.

"Keep an eye out for a slender man. Square-shouldered. He rides a mousy gray mustang and mounts from the Indian side. Got an orange dog with him."

Fipps nodded. "They came through late yesterday and wound back this way not two hours ago heading toward Rough and Ready. You ought to have passed them."

To himself, Reuben admitted bitterly that he was being jerked about in Jasper's cat-and-mouse game and was tired of being the mouse, but he had no remedy for it. None short of catching up with Jasper and shutting the game down. "Ed, how did this Wah Gung die?"

"Well, that was peculiar. Sheriff Kritch found hardly a mark on him. Just a little wound at the base of his skull. But he was murdered right enough and in his sleep. Family all around him and nobody heard a thing."

11

By the first gray light of morning, Maxine had cleared the table of dishes used in Reuben's hasty breakfast and secured her outside doors with wooden wedges, the keys having long been lost and not replaced. Staring out of the parlor window, she thought more than half a lifetime back of how she'd taken up with Charlie, married the young deputy much against her mother's wishes, and how the marriage had not, as her mother predicted, paid off in money. The memory of the clashes she had with her mother brought a brief smile to her face because she had been paid in contentment, and that was something that money had never bought her mother.

All this she pushed aside. Her protector, her contentment provider was laid up in bed, and Jasper Chase was on the loose. Odds were he would wait until night, but he was sure to return. So Maxine had to wait and worry. Worry about a bedbound Charlie. Worry about Reuben somewhere on Jasper's trail and Carl, helpless at the top of Doc Schmelling's rickety stairs. All were vulnerable until Jasper was stopped, and try as she might, she could not in all her Methodist soul wish him any better than a quick death.

And worry she did, but she couldn't leave the house; Jasper might come while she was gone. Chores would help. She prepared a careful breakfast for Charlie and saw to his needs. When not caring for him, she nervously cleaned house top to bottom, and still the long day stretched before her. Later she struggled through an afternoon nap that was filled with frightful dreams. Still no Jasper. No Reuben.

12

Reuben stared down the road to Rough and Ready, the road he'd just come. If the big games were downtown and the table Wah Gung ran was an honest one, then Wah Gung was blameless and his death was needless. And now Jasper had turned back toward the Springs. Was he checking to see if his brothers were still alive? Was he returning to finish Charlie off?

"Damn it, Fipps. This changes everything. Let's get that saddle on the bay. I'll trail the roan. I've got to hurry back the way I came. Missed him on the trail. It's likely he watched me ride by."

What he didn't say was that everyone he felt close to and anyone that Jasper was likely to attack, himself excepted, was back at Whistling Springs. Worst was, he had to come all this way to learn that.

Minutes later, he had the bay on the trail, the roan following, but it was a six-hour ride to the Springs, and Jasper had better than a two-hour lead. The bay could make up some time, but however they did it, they had to make it before dark fell, before Jasper struck again.

While Reuben was dominated by the need to return quickly to Whistling Springs, Maxine was fretting. For two weeks, Jasper's presence had rubbed her nerves raw. Now his absence, the not knowing just where he was, she found to be worse. It made her broody as a setting hen. She began compulsively to clean the living room again. In the process, she spotted Tor Jenns's wood wagon in the alley behind the neighbor's house. The man was carelessly heaving wood into Mrs. Appleby's flower bed. That was not at all like Tor. She moved to a darkened room to avoid being seen and watched the figure throwing wood. He stopped his labors and appeared to mop at his face with a handkerchief, but he was staring all the while at the bed visible in her parlor window. It was a chilling sight for Maxine. The wagon and the team were Tor's, and the clothing was Tor's, but it was not Tor under the floppy black hat. It was Jasper Chase.

Moments later, apparently satisfied with what he'd seen, Jasper and the wood wagon were gone.

For a few moments, Maxine was indecisive, even fearful. It was not fear for herself but for Charlie. With Jasper within easy rifle shot of her parlor window, the odds seemed to be stacked against her. Still, with any luck, Jasper would stick to what worked for him: some kind of attack in the dark of night.

She sat at the bottom of her living room stairs until most of the light had left the western sky then set a light by the bay window, brought a white washbasin and a towel from the kitchen and went through the motions of bathing her husband. Jasper might be watching from somewhere.

Jasper's first impulse when he saw Charlie Prescott's cot by the window was to shoot him where he lay. But he had a better method, one that had served him well before, one that was quiet and gave him the cover of night. He'd stick with that.

Night had fallen on Reuben and the big bay but not before the lights of the Springs could be seen. Another half mile. Reuben urged the bay to a last effort.

Supper over in the houses about town and lights on in parlors, Whistling Springs was settling into the evening. It was Jasper's time. He made his quiet way into Maxine's kitchen. Once in, he allowed a count of fifty to elapse between each step. Soundlessly, laboriously, he crept to the parlor door from where he could see the white-clad form near the window. More time and once again, laboriously, one step and a count of fifty. Even if a board were to squeak, it would sound like nothing more than the old house giving off the heat of the day. Finally at the bedside, he slipped the folding knife from his pocket and opened it only to discover that the sickbed was filled with pillows.

A slight sound, hardly more than the rustle of a mouse in straw, woke Maxine, and as Jasper turned back to the middle of the room. The pale gray light of the gibbous moon broke through a curtain of clouds, spilled into the garden and through the filmy curtains on the bay window. It gave Maxine his silhouette. When he heard the snick, snick of hammers, Jasper took two steps and launched himself over the bed and through the parlor window.

Fully awake in an instant, Maxine raised partway out of her chair and, with the instinctive aim of a bird hunter, swung and fired the first barrel without sighting, then reached with her finger for the second. On target now, she pulled with deliberation.

The first barrel tore a piece out of Jasper's left shoulder. The second charge was late and finished tearing the glass out of the top of the parlor window. With shaking hands, she fumbled in her apron pocket for reloads.

Jasper landed heavily on the side yard's paving stones, but leery of Maxine's shotgun, he quickly rolled to his feet and struggled toward the alley and the mustang he'd picketed near the neighbor's woodpile. A terrible pain coursed through his left shoulder, a freshet of sticky blood was soaking his shirt.

Thoughts rolled in faster than the waves of pain. *The old bitch has caught me fair and square, but I ain't through. She thinks she's outsmarted me. Got the old man upstairs and thinks he's safe. Well, she can burn with him.* He made straight to her woodshed and returned to the corner of the house with wood scraps. *They don't have me licked. Once the fire is goin' good, I'll mount up, and the mustang'll take me outta here. Then it can burn. All of it. The whole damn town.*

The first match, pulled out of his shirt pocket, failed to light. There were more matches, but they were in his left jeans pocket. He had to fish them out with his right hand. Precious seconds passed. Where was the woman with the shotgun? He got a match clear of the pocket but dropped it. When he fell to his knees in search of it, he heard Braddock's cold command, "Hands high, Jasper Chase. You're wanted for murder."

It had to be the big deputy's voice, and in that instant Jasper had a vision, not of the home place with the meadows full of cattle, not of Bear Valley and the dark-eyed Juanita, and not even of the deputy who called him out, but a vision of the cold stone walls of Folsom Prison. There was but one choice. "No. No," he shouted. "I'll see you in hell first." He turned slowly, almost indifferently, then with a quick dip of his shoulder clawed at his holster. Before he cleared leather, he saw twin belches of fire from Reuben's pistol. A sear of lead tore his gun arm, another his chest. Jasper fell away, his pistol dangling heavily from a hand gone nerveless. His eyes lost focus. He fell forward over his Colt.

Moments later, Maxine emerged from her house carrying a lantern and the sixteen gauge. She held the lantern while Reuben turned over the corpse of Jasper Chase.

Next morning, they had Charlie propped up in his chair in the kitchen, the parlor awaiting repairs. Reuben was having coffee with the Prescotts, the mayor, and the bank president, Gabe Cassel.

Cassel spoke, "The town is plumb pleased, Reuben, but short of cash. We found money on Jasper, used it to bury him. Also bought train tickets for you and your two horses. And, since Charlie says you're rough on horses, we are giving you Chase's mustang and a train ticket for it as well. Since you're anxious to move on, we'll take care of other details."

"Don't forget Jasper's dog."

"Don't worry about that old dog," said Charlie. "Maxine's made a bed for him in the woodshed."

PART TWO

1

Reuben peered out the window of the Southern Pacific's best car. They were far up the mountain now approaching the snowsheds at Norden and would soon be working their way down the Nevada side of the Sierras. His immediate neighbors were a drummer in a gone-shabby brown suit and an army corporal on furlough. They were playing two-handed solitaire. He had just avoided a "friendly hand of poker" with the pair but, not to seem unfriendly, had passed around the "going away" bottle of whiskey given him by Charlie Prescott. As the bottle came around a second time, he waved it away, left it to them. They got back into their game, and Reuben once more succumbed to the klak-a-t-klak of the rails, but instead of drifting into sleep, his thoughts went back to the days following the shootout at Carlson Creek Bridge, back to his rescue by the widow Justus and how that was all hooked into an afternoon in Charlie Prescott's office. There they talked about the job of keeping the peace and how Reuben's father had summed it up, saying, "It's the lawman's dilemma. Your job is to move to a lawless town, make it safe to live in, and then move on to one that ain't."

Reuben had given that much thought, and it seemed to him that such talk was as much about settling down as it was about keeping the law. The "settling down" part was gnawing at Reuben now as he stared out the window, not seeing the great granite boulders, the lakes, and the trees, not seeing the day fade into night. He was seeing instead clearly and sadly into the past, a past in which he'd had the chance to settle and had made a mess of it, had what he wanted and didn't realize it. He'd somehow avoided telling Charlie about Willa and hadn't told Maxine either, which was a wonder because she could pry a story out of a rock.

2

Willa Justus poked up the fire in the woodstove. She was heating bathwater. To hell with how hot the kitchen would become, she had hay itch on just about every part of her body. The fire stirred to her satisfaction, she wheeled her bathtub close to the stove to make ladling water less a chore. The tub was her joy. Number 16405 in the Sears catalog, it was a full six feet in length and japanned blue inside with handles at each end for portability. It sported three stripes on the outside, one of them gilt, and had cost her three prime steers but was worth every bit of it. She could stretch her whole length into it with just a bit to spare. She shook her head remembering the years she'd spent trying to get clean in a washtub and—

There came a knocking at the kitchen door. The hired man had finished putting up the horses and wanted his pay. Good. The hay was finished, and now she could pay him off, get rid of him. Him and his nosey eyes. He was a neighbor to the south and handy help with the heavy work. But he had aggravated her, and he was doing it again. Though he stood hat in hand in the doorway that tied her kitchen to the screened porch and though he appeared to be waiting (the perfect picture of the humble servant) simply for his wages, his busy eyes took in the kettles and water buckets heating on the stove, took in her fancy bathtub, and they were taking her in as well. He was trying to picture her easing into the tub. Perhaps he was comparing her with the stringy, worn-out little mouse he'd left back at his cabin.

Willa easily read his mind, every untidy, ungentlemanly corner of it. In her frostiest voice she said, "Here's your pay, Mr. Swinch." He held out his hands. "I won't keep you but a moment more. Wash day, isn't it? And a storm brewing. You'll want to hurry home and give your wife a hand. And the kids . . . How many now? Six, isn't it? But first . . ." His hands still outstretched, she let him stand that way and wait. She caught his eye then and held it. "You're a good hay hand and tolerable good around a woodlot, Mr. Swinch, but I can't trust you. Caught you sneaking looks at me when we were haying, and just now you were at it again. I purely won't have it. If you *ever* get asked to work here again, you'll know to keep your eyes and your thoughts to yourself. That understood?" He looked down at his shoes, nodded. She waited to be sure it sunk in, then added, "Some men, Mr. Swinch, are of the opinion that widow ladies, especially young ones, ought to be accommodating. I ain't one of them." She was annoyed and stayed that way. Wasn't it enough that hay chaff and dust worked its way under her clothes? Did she have to put up with a nosey-eyed Swinch trying to do the same? She supposed she wasn't dressed strictly modest, but to be so, she'd have to pile on the under gear, dress like a preacher's wife. You'd play hell trying to harvest hay burdened down like that. And so after paying him his wages, not trusting him, she waited under the big live oak by the back door and watched until he disappeared homeward.

Sure of his departure now, she called Tip, all-purpose cattle dog and burglar alarm, into the kitchen. She fished around in the bean pot now warming with the bathwater until she found a piece of bacon rind used to season the beans. She piled the rind and hot beans onto the bread scraps already in his pan. All this done, she ate a small dish of beans and sipped coffee while the water finished heating.

The task of filling her fancy tub from the buckets on the stove completed, Willa added a splash of lavender to the water, stripped off her sweaty clothes, and slipped into the tub. Submerged in hot water to her chin, she lazed back and listened to the approach of the summer storm. It had been just a distant warning rumble in the early afternoon (enough to hustle them through the last load of hay). It came in rush now, drenching the hay meadow, working its way to the horse pasture, the barn lot, the garden spot and finally slamming into the side of her house. Willa snuggled deeper into the tub and congratulated herself on the timing of the hay harvest. Soreness, weariness washing away, she relaxed. The calves were worked, the hay was in, the woodshed full; she could settle into an easy routine of housekeeping and garden tending. Better yet, she could give the horses a day to rest, then go to town, visit friends, stay a night in the hotel, buy a new dress. Looked at that way, she had about everything a woman would want—except a man.

She had begun to think along those lines when Tip awoke. Hackles raised, he rushed to the door barking. "Hush, you, Tip. Hush." She listened. *Oh, crap. Someone in the yard. Just when you've got things on a downhill pull . . .*

The knock came before Willa could wiggle out of the tub. She eased out, toweled briefly, and shrugged into her robe, fished with her feet until they found slippers. She pulled her shotgun off the kitchen table and approached the door. *If it's that damn Swinch nosing around, I'm gonna dust his britches.* More horses in the yard now and the pound of heavy boots on her porch. More men. The knock became insistent. "Willa, are you in there? It's Sheriff Jody King."

"Yeh, keep your shirt on." With the barrel of the ancient shotgun, she lifted the door latch and looked through the gap at the group on her little porch.

"Willa, I got a deputy bad hurt. Can't take him clear to town."

"That my root cellar door you got him on?"

"Stopped at Mrs. Hodges. Got it there."

"Whyn't you leave the deputy with her?"

"Leave him there? She's got a houseful of kids. Can we come in?"

Willa took over. Gesturing to the two men carrying the body, she said, "Put your deputy on the cot under the window. Jody, you poke up the fire, somebody light another lamp. I'll bring blankets. We gotta get his temperature back up, get Doc Seevers."

"I sent a man for the doc an hour back. Be here soon."

She came back from her bedroom with a wool blanket and a light quilt. "What'd he break?"

"It ain't a break. He's shot up."

"Shot? Will you men step back out uh my light! Get yourself some beans and coffee but stay outta my way.

"Now, Jody, we gotta cut these wet clothes off him, get at the wounds."

Soon as he was settled and the bleeding stopped, she pulled the sheriff aside. "I don't like his color, and I don't like you bringing him here."

"No, ma'am. I do hate to bother you, but I couldn't take him on into town."

"What you're not telling me, Jody, is that you don't think he'll make it. Don't want him dying on your hands."

"No, ain't that, Willa. I ask ya, what kinda care is he gonna get in town? Go to Seevers's 'hospital'? 'Sides, he's all broke up. We were afraid to move him this far."

"You owe me, Jody King. And I will collect."

It was late afternoon of the third day in Willa's warm kitchen that Reuben struggled to bring himself around. It was like trying to swim in heavy water. He stayed on top long enough to see that he was in a sunny room, that the curtains at the window billowed in and out as though the house was breathing. He was vaguely aware of a soft voice and the scent of lavender. An angel was changing his dressings, holding a cool cloth to his forehead. He drifted off.

She came in late one night in answer to his restless moaning. Moonlight through the window bathed her in a soft light. "Alma? That you, Alma?"

"No. I'm Wilhamena Justus. People call me Willa."

For the first time since his battle on the Carlson Creek Bridge, he felt clearheaded enough to talk. "I'm Reuben Braddock. I—"

She hushed him. "Save your energy, Reuben. Sheriff King brought you here. Said you'd picked up some lead in your hip and shoulder and couldn't risk taking you clear to town. Doc Seevers came and pried out the lead, left you in my care. That was nearly a week back." She paused, considering how much to tell him. "I can tell you now, I was pretty upset with the sheriff. Figured he'd dumped you in my lap to die. There were days I thought that too."

"Glad to see you changed your mind."

"Hmm. This Alma you asked for . . . ?"

"I was asking for Alma? She was my best friend's older sister. I was thirteen or fourteen then and pretty sure I was in love with her."

"So there's no lady wondering where you are?"

"No, not for some time now." He was tired, surprised how quickly the talking wore him down, but he managed to say, "Thanks, Willa, for saving my hide," before drifting off again.

Several more days passed while Reuben gained strength. Broth became soup; the soups became thicker and finally gave way to venison stew. He was on the mend, was up part of the day looking out the window. Reuben looked forward to her coming, loved the feel of her hands, loved the sight of her for she was willowy, with soft, mature curves and a wealth of chestnut hair she wore tied back. The angel was a real, live, warm woman.

A week later, a week in which Reuben made great strides toward recovery, a thunderstorm rumbled across the foothills, rattled the windows and doors, and sent the willows along the creek into a shivering dance. The parched earth opened to receive the rain. Reuben was vaguely aware of its rumbling, slept fitfully, dreamed, and called out.

Willa had moved him into the spare room; she came to him there bearing a coal oil lamp. She was wearing a flannel shift and had let loose her chestnut hair. Placing the lamp on the table near the bed, she checked her patient. "Just what I figured, you've kicked off half your blankets." She fussed with the covers, tucked them under his chin. "You're cold, Reuben, and . . ." Whatever she had intended to say next got lost as a contrary notion intruded. It was a notion she had fought off. She had joined his bed before, but he'd been close onto death then, and the warmth she took to him was medicinal, and if it served in some way to ease a pain of her own, that was a bonus. But this was different. *Lord help us,* she thought. *Where's a preacher when you need him?*

"You know what, Reuben? This waiting on ceremony is all nonsense. It's time you started earning your keep around here." So saying, she pulled up the covers and slid in against his back. He was fully awake now, and the heat she brought astonished him. He waited another few moments, her body pulling all the cold out of him, replacing it with an urgency. He turned toward her.

"The light," he murmured.

"Let it burn, Reuben. I'm hungry. Been hungry ever so long . . . Let it burn."

3

A year passed, and their second summer blended dreamlike into fall. They put up hay, worked the calves, got in the winter wood, and shared a bed. Reuben seemed at home, comfortable and settled, until the letter came.

After he read it, he asked Willa to ride to the meadow with him. Side by side they took the ridge trail behind the barn. It was her favorite ride down through the black oak and digger pine, the oaks now changing to browns and golds, the digger pines standing tall and gaunt, looking like gray survivors from another time.

They rode to the center of the hay meadow and into the shade of the spreading valley oaks. Once they were settled, he searched for her hand. "I need to talk to you about the letter I got this morning. It's a chance for us to make a good piece of money."

"The place takes care of us," she replied.

"Things come up. Illnesses, opportunities. We could buy a little stock, improve the herd."

"I don't see it," she said. "Grandfather built this herd, and it suits the country. Suits me."

He had been staring out across the meadow as they spoke as though he were looking at something somewhere else. She'd seen that look before. Seen it on her father's face. It was a restless, wandering sort of look. Wandering had taken over her father's life, led to her mother's death. She had feared its onset in Reuben, had tried to steel herself against it. Now here it was, and she had to deal with it.

She pulled herself onto his lap, took his face in her two hands, compelling him to look at her. "What's in the letter, Reuben?"

Any further effort to evade the issue was impossible. "It's an offer to sheriff over Colorado way. Good pay and we'll be right back here in a year's time, safe and sound. Money ahead." He said it all in a rush and looked away again.

Sliding off his lap, she shook her head slowly and sadly. "You'll have to go alone, Reuben. I won't go wandering. There would be no cattle when we got back, and it's likely that one of my good neighbors would have moved onto my land, into my house. I can't go and . . ." She trailed off and was quiet a moment before she continued, frustrated and angry. "And I can't be stuck wondering when they'll bring you to me half dead again. It's not as though we need the money. We have everything we need right here. And, Reuben . . . this thing we have together, well never find again . . . neither of us."

"I'll cut it short, be back for spring calving. I promise."

"That'd be nice, but you won't."

A hawk flew over. Quail called from a thicket of blackberries. A breeze rustled the treetops. Reuben searched for the right reply. Couldn't find it. The hawk circled over the blackberry patch. She rose, brushed off her dress. Now she was looking at something far off. "They are right, you know. Way leads onto way, Reuben. Way leads onto way." She felt a numbness settling in, fled to her horse, galloped away without a look back.

He'd thrown up a barrier between them. The next morning, he tried to put into words what pulled at him. "It's like a preacher's calling," he said. "A town asks for help and I answer. It was my father's calling and his father's before him. Just this one year, Willa. Less even, and I'll be back. Back to stay."

She kissed him good-bye, but she was angry. She watched until he dropped out of sight behind a ridge. The screen door banged shut behind her as she entered the kitchen. It seemed cold. She built up the fire and sat staring at the wood box.

4

A year went by, then nearly two before Reuben once again sat his horse high on the ridge above Willa's. Unsure of his welcome, he hesitated on the digger pine hillside, ran his glass over the farm. Nothing seemed changed; smoke rose peacefully from the chimney of the little house, and sounds of chopping came from the woodshed. Willa had never been very skillful at chopping wood. Maybe if he rode into the yard, chopped some wood for her, filled the wood box, he'd get asked to lunch, get a chance to apologize, another chance to explain his calling. She might even welcome him back.

While he was pondering these matters, Willa came out of the house cradling a small bundle. The chopping stopped, and a man walked out of the woodshed shadows to greet her, peered into the blanket.

Willa had moved on, had shut the door to the past. An unexpected wave of anger swept over Reuben, anger at first directed at Willa but soon tempered as he realized that somewhere deep down and against all reason, he'd expected to be welcomed back no matter how tardy; he had counted on it. What he felt wasn't anger; it was regret. He'd been a fool. Willa's words came rushing back to him: "What we have together we will never find again. Neither of us."

Reuben, as you know, moved on to face the trouble at Whistling Springs, but he was not soon to forget Willa's words and the bitter taste in his mouth that he figured came from the lawman's dilemma.

PART THREE

Showdown at Morning Glory Wells

1

The train was late arriving at Silvercrown. Reuben had to roust the livery boy to get the horses settled, then pound at the hotel front desk to get a room for himself. He was up early the next morning eager to push the past aside and eager for the challenge ahead at Elder Creek. By the time he called in at the sheriff's office, walked about town, bought some new duds, and checked on his horses, he was tired and declared the next day the travel day. He soaked in the hotel tub until dinnertime. Dinner was roast beef with carrots and potatoes, a side of apples and cabbage. He topped it with a full night of sleep in a feather bed. He was going home to Elder Creek, and he wanted to look on the neat and prosperous side.

Three hours after leaving the railhead at Silvercrown and a half mile by crow flight from Elder Creek, Braddock left the road and urged the bay up a gentle ridge. He dismounted in a clump of piñon pines. The morning fog that had clung along the river and in the hollows between the hills had burned off, and the trees were clear of frost. He shucked his great coat and tied it onto the gray mustang. He trailed the gray mustang and a sorrel mare. Some would consider him horse poor.

He fished a spyglass out of his saddlebag and used it to survey Elder Creek. Memories began to flood in. It had been a dozen years since he'd walked those streets, visited friends, fished the river. The red brick of the bank still anchored the town on the left as you entered from the south. At the other end of the business street, the little school where he'd learned to read and do sums was still there just past Boot Hill. It was home as he remembered it, but somehow the town looked smaller, the houses more scattered. He should have expected that; things grow in the telling, loom larger in memory. Things looked so quiet, orderly. What was going on in Elder Creek that had the town fathers all in a lather? Why had they called him?

He ran his glass north of the Military Road toward the Ketchum Mine. There were fresh memories wherever he looked. Even now, the Alvordo's broad expanses, its stark and awful beauty pulled at him. "What do you say, little horse? It's been a long time since I rode out there. When we get a few days off, we'll visit my old camp under the Keller Rim. Right now, we'd best check in. Let the town know we're here."

The first house in town was a Mexican-style adobe that was new to him. Perched on a slight mound between the road and the river, it was partly shielded from the Ridge Road by a row of cottonwood trees. There was a garden beside the adobe with young corn plants covered with gallon jugs and set wide apart and haphazardly as though not planted with care. He knew better. It was Indian corn and planted that way to take advantage of what moisture there was. There were carrot and other root crops planted in regular rows. Lettuce and radishes too. It looked neat, well tended. Then he saw the tender, watched her tuck a stray lock of black hair under a wide-brimmed straw hat.

He dismounted and walked the horse within a few feet of her stone wall. Dismounting, it seemed to him, made you look less threatening. He doffed his hat. "Excuse me, ma'am. I'm your new marshal and just wonderin' where they might have put the mayor's office. I need to report in."

She shaded her eyes, came closer to the fence. She was wearing a dark-blue skirt to her ankles and a white short-sleeved blouse. When she looked up, he caught full sight of her startling brown eyes, dark and gold flecked. Her skin was warm and appealing in the noon light. He stifled a sudden urge to go closer, to touch her. He thought little of his impulse at the time, figured he was just glad to be home. She spoke then, "You're the Braddock Boy they've been talking about." She stopped and openly took in the length of him, the heavily muscled arms, the broad shoulders. She laughed. "Seems to me there's been some years since they've seen you, Marshal Braddock."

"Reuben, ma'am."

"Reuben then. I'm Maria, Maria Vasguez. You'll find the mayor at the blacksmith shop. And, Reuben, I imagine that you are in a hurry now, so I won't keep you, but please feel welcome to stop by. I run a little café open noon to about six or so. Come visit when you've got more time. I'm most usually here."

"I'll be sure to do so, Maria." He looked beyond her at the garden. "That sweet corn I see?"

"My corn is for flour if the frost doesn't get it. For tortillas."

"You keep a nice garden." He mounted, tipped his hat, and clucked at the bay.

She watched as he rode off. A new man in town. A big man.

Maria had come to Elder Creek by way of Mexico, where she was born, and El Paso, where her family lived for many years and where she met her husband, Louis. She wondered sometimes at the way it happened. None of it seeming to be in her control. Her father, Martin Goetz, was a mining engineer of German descent, and her mother was the beautiful Dolores Alcizar Escondido of Monterey.

Life in El Paso had been pleasant for Maria. Her parents sent her to school where she had good friends, but life changed radically when her father died in a tunnel collapse at the E1 Hombre Rico mine. Her mother remarried, but the new father, civil and kind at first, turned out to be an abusive, miserly wretch. Maria escaped him into the arms of Louis de Camba Vasguez. Her mother dismissively described Louis as "a very ordinary man with a classic name. You will have marvelous children." But the children never happened. She and Louis drifted north, finally finding steady work driving ore wagons for the Ketchum Mine. They had two happy years building their home, then came a dispute at the mine, and Louis was dead, killed in a cross fire. Friends helped her open the café.

2

Reuben trailed his horses up Main Street toward its northern end where the blacksmith shop had been. The town looked peaceful. On the left side was the substantial brick of Elder Creek's bank, the sprawling buildings of the freight yard, and then the blacksmith shop itself.

On his right hand was the assay office boarded up now with a faded and cobwebbed Closed sign in its window. The Mountain View saloon, sporting a few horses at the hitch rack, looked unchanged. A newly painted sign declaring Gunnison's Mercantile was the lone hint of prosperity on the street. Next to it was the modest two-story Little Willow Hotel. He'd put up there. Under its awning swung a small sign with an arrow pointing up the side stairs that simply said Doc Miller.

The town *was* smaller. There once was a street full of businesses that sat between Main Street and the river. An outgrowth of Elder Creek's boom days, at one time, that street boasted a half dozen saloons and a pair of sporting houses all constructed of rough-sawed lumber. On that same street had been rows of tents housing temporary restaurants and flophouses. Now the only remaining building on that street appeared to be a Chinese laundry. The rest were gone almost without a trace. He had never walked that street as a youth for fear his mother would hear he'd been there.

A rhythmic tap, tap, tap of a small hammer on metal led him to the blacksmith shop. Some delicate work? A cross for a young girl's necklace? He tied the horses to the hitch rack. After a bit, his eyes adjusted to the gloom, and he saw the smith.

The smith stopped his work and came forward, his hand out. "I'm Tap Trundle, and you'd be Reuben Braddock. It's good to see you, Reuben. I knew your folks before they moved to Reno. I think you were sheriff then in some town in California."

"That'd be about right. Pleased to meet you, Tap." He looked at the contents of the shop: stacks of iron, bellows, forge, a round of wood with an anvil mounted at convenient height, a small table with a coffeepot and a kerosene lantern. On the dirt floor near the table stood a pair of wooden barrels, one empty and one half full of handmade nails. The barrels explained the light tapping sound. Trundle was filling his time making nails, a sure sign that business was slow. Reuben turned his attention back to Trundle. "This place was run by Wally Shems when I was last here. What happened to Wally?"

"Wally is my uncle on my mother's side. He sorta wore out, sold me the shop. He's got a little place here in town with a garden, coupla dogs. Keeps him happy. You look rested, Reuben."

"I came by train to Silvercrown. Stayed in a hotel. Ate fancy grub. But living like that could make a man lazy."

"It's good you're rested. A person can't predict how much a that he'll get around here. You'll be wanting to move into your office. The Mountain View Gang burned down the building we gave Sheriff Carney, so I got the freight company to give up the southwest corner of their place. It's better than Carney had, with a good view of the street but no jail cells as yet. Pay is forty dollars a month until I can get them to raise it."

"Who should I ask for down there?"

"Suppose I go with you. It'd be my pleasure to show you around a little, and since the banker, Rolly Hodges, owns the freight company too, we might as well make him the first call."

"Counting you, it'll be the third call. I leaned over the fence and talked with Mrs. Vasguez on my way in."

"Widow Vasguez. They had some trouble over at the Ketchum Mine a year back. Her husband was killed in the fracas."

"That's a damn shame. Nice lady like that widowed."

Trundle took off his leather apron. "We'll let the fire die down a bit then go see that banker."

"So, Tap, the town seemed awful anxious to get me here. What do they expect me to do?"

"As I suspect you know, Elder Creek has a rowdy past, and although the dance hall girls and the gamblers have mostly left town, a small pesky gang of thieves remains. Heavily armed and quarrelsome, they rule the little town, forcing businesses and some homeowners to buy 'protection.' The gang was easier to overlook during the boom, but now businesses are hard-pressed to keep their doors open. The 'protection' money takes a fearsome bite. Things weren't bad enough, I guess. Next thing we knew, our sheriff met with an 'accident' on a trail north of here. Bushwhacked, I'd say. Nothing we could prove."

"This protection racket . . . ?"

"If you don't pay 'fire insurance,' they burn you out."

"Let's go see that office."

3

Headquarters of the Rocking R sat on a bench overlooking Grizzly Creek Meadows. It was a good-size spread with subirrigated hay land, high country for summer grazing. It carried three hired hands busy with cattle, hay, and miles of fence. Though the fence rankled some of the old-timers who called it a newfangled nuisance, most cattlemen grudgingly accepted it as the wave of the future. New also to the Rocking R was Vance Wagner. A bank robbery gone bad in Kansas and a shooting in Colorado had put him on the Wanted posters. He had fled to Elder Creek to take the heat off. With only one road connecting the town to the outside world, it seemed ideal. He camped near the road for a few days and watched his back trail. When everything looked calm enough, he'd taken a cow-punching job at the Rocking R. By the time Reno Rawlins, owner of the spread, realized that he'd hired a gunslinger instead of a cowman, Wagner had brawled his way into leadership in the bunkhouse. Reluctantly, Rawlins named him foreman.

Gainfully employed and settled out of the way, Wagner should have been content, but he was a restless man. Most evenings in the Rocking R bunkhouse, the hands sat about the table playing cribbage and telling stories. This was not enough for Wagner. He yearned for the poker table, the company of dance hall women.

His dependence on the dance hall girls came to light one Friday in early spring. That morning, he made some excuse at the ranch and rode in to have it out with Miss Candyce Lyle. Pounding up the stairs at the Mountain View two at a time, he banged furiously at her door. She had not made herself available to him for their usual Wednesday night date, hadn't worked Thursday night either.

"Candy, it's Vance."

"I'm not seeing anyone, Vance. Just go away."

"Quit foolin' around, Candy. We gotta talk." He returned to his furious pounding on the door. Paused and called to her again, "Candy?"

"Just a moment then. I swear you'd wake the dead with your pounding." There was a rattling of a chain. She threw the door wide open and stood aside as she did so. Instead of the frilly little something or other he expected to find her in, she was dressed to travel. He was surprised, speechless.

She was a tall woman, slim of waist, red haired and green eyed. Dressed to travel, she was a head-turner no matter what city she was in. This day she was in no mood to cater to Wagner. "You got something to say, make it snappy. I was expecting the swamper to carry my trunk downstairs. Instead, you show up."

She didn't seem glad to see him. There was a pause while he tried to digest what he saw. "Well, don't just stand there gawking," she said. "What's to talk about?"

"Us."

"Us? Vance, there is no 'us.' I've just been a cheap convenience for you. It's like I told you last week, Veronica and I are the last 'girls' in town. The others left a long time ago, and we should have left with them."

"Why, there's the miners and a new mine opening soon. You'll have loads of customers."

"A new mine opening soon. I expect that I've heard that a dozen times in the last month and twice that in the month before. As for the miners that are here, they're mostly married and Cousin Jacks to boot. They're as tight as a new corset. Can't you see it? The town's dead. And you know something, Vance? The stage is down to one run a week. A Friday run. This is Friday and we're running."

One thing people learned early about Vance Wagner: there wasn't an ounce of humor in him. "You can't do this to me."

"To you? Can't? I have to." She stopped and stared at him a long minute. Impatiently she continued, "I can see that this puts you in a panic. You were in a panic when you first came to me, remember? Seems like you need someone to lean on."

"I really like you, Candy."

"Uh-huh. Truth is, you panic when you don't 'have a woman.' Your words. You told me that yourself. We had some good moments, but that is not sufficient reason for me to stay in this town. I can't be 'your woman.' So get over it."

Wagner had maintained his position between Candy and the door, blocking her exit from the room. Now he reached out to grab her. With a quickness that surprised him, she backed off and whipped a small nickel-plated revolver out of her bag.

"Out of my way, Vance. Nothing you can do or say will change things. I'm going slow broke in Elder Creek. Maybe worse than slow."

"Where ya goin'?"

"Move your carcass over to that chair and keep your hands where I can see them and I'll tell you." She put the pistol in her purse but left her hand in with it. He sat on the edge of the chair and threw his right leg over his left in what he hoped was a posture of nonchalance. "It'll be Denver, Vance. Not that it matters. You are not likely to come visit, and the way you push people around, you've got Boot Hill written all over you."

Her green silk skirt swirling about her ankles, she danced out the door. He heard the creak of the stairs as she descended them. He looked about at the paintless window frames, the scrap of worn red rug. Except for her scarred leather-bound trunk, the cheap cast iron bed, and the straight-backed chair he sat in, the room was empty and cheerless. Whatever had made it seem bright and warm was gone. She was leaving and to Denver at that. Might as well be the moon. He was on Wanted posters all over the state of Colorado.

Vance felt indignant and betrayed. He followed Candyce to the lobby. Meeting the swamper on the stairwell, he angrily slammed the man into the wall as he passed him. In the lobby he saw that Veronica was ready to travel as well. She was in a sky blue dress that set off her eyes and a black cloak that matched her hair. She was a small woman with rounded, subtle curves that she made no effort to hide. Her trunk and valise were neatly arranged near the lobby door. The women were having a lively conversation and had found something to laugh about. Wagner felt left out. When he had money in his hand and Candy was dressed to entertain, he felt confident and at ease. Why did things have to change?

He looked at the two women. Dressed as they were, with the chance to fly off to a new beginning, they had about them an aura of freedom and sophistication that angered him. As he strode by Candy, he made eye contact with her. There was no sympathy there. Instead, Candy kept her right hand in her bag and wrapped around the revolver until he was out the door.

Powerless to stop her and furious at himself that he cared whether she left or stayed, he set spurs to his horse and galloped up the street. At the outskirts of town, a skinny black dog crossed his path. The fury in him welled up. In one smooth motion he pulled his gun, fired, and rode on without a backward look at the gut-shot dog.

As the days went by, Vance found Elder Creek to be more curse than blessing. He'd come to the conclusion that it was quiet enough to hide in, but too quiet to live in. He was lonely, missed the visits to the woman's room. It had given him a comfort that he looked forward to, and maybe he had told her the truth. Maybe he did like her. It didn't matter now. She was gone.

4

Braddock's office sported a pair of small windows looking onto the street and a pair of barrel-backed chairs pulled up to a sturdy desk. He had decorated two of the walls with Wanted posters. In the corner away from the door was a potbellied stove with a scuttle of coal nearby. There was no fire now as the noon sun was pleasantly streaming through his windows. A small room at the rear held his cot and a shaving stand with a washbasin and a mirror. It went with the job. As Tap had mentioned, there were no cells. Prisoners were held in a root cellar.

Braddock was seated at the desk reading Wanted posters that had arrived by that morning's stage when Tap Trundle came in off the street. Tap had an unlikely build for a blacksmith. His heavily muscled shoulders and arms sat improbably atop a slender waist and long thin legs. He was blessed with a great shock of brown hair and dancing brown eyes. He was wearing clean jeans, a collarless shirt, and a waist-length leather jacket in place of the usual leather apron. His high-topped boots were laced to just under the knee.

Like a schoolboy on a picnic, he had bounce to his step, a smile on his friendly face.

"Hello, Tap. Things treating you all right?"

"Things are all right, Reuben. No use complaining. I came in to remind you that the stage leaves about three o'clock. If you like, I'd go with you and help identify any local characters who might be departing. There was one drummer on the stage when it rolled in at noon. He's been at the mercantile and is likely to leave at three with the rest of 'em."

"Thank you. Keeping track might come in handy someday. I'm lookin' at Wanted posters right now." He pointed to an array on the wall. "Anyone there you know?"

After a quick look, Tap declared, "Nobody on these. Reason I mention the stage is because the last of the dance hall girls will be leavin' on it."

"I'll go with you to see them off, but just to finish this thought, look at the posters on my desk too. I find it interesting that none come from Colorado and only one from Idaho, for that matter."

"That is strange, Reuben. Maybe Billings at the post office is holding 'em back. You can't tell me there's no trouble over there. As for Elder Creek, it's surprising the folks that don't get their face on a poster. You look at Pelham and his gang at the Mountain View, and then there's Wagner. He oughta be on somebody's poster. Wears his gun low and tied down and carries a reputation. At least he says he does. Earned or not, I keep my eye on him."

:Is he part of the gang?"

"Not now. Maybe he wants to be. He came in a several months back. Supposed to be foreman out at the Rocking R, but I see him at the Mountain View a mite frequent for a cowhand."

"Now that you mention it, he came out of the Mountain View just a half hour back. Rode off north."

"He was sweet on one of the girls."

"That so? And you say they're leaving today? He just might double back. Cause some trouble."

Braddock got up, slapped on his hat, and tightened his gun belt. "Let's go to the livery. You can ride my bay. If you've got time, we'll escort the stage the first three or four miles out the Ridge Road. When we get back, we'll stop for pie and coffee at Maria's."

"Pie and coffee, Reuben? I'd be a fool to refuse."

When Tap and Reuben arrived, Candy and Veronica were waiting in front of the Mountain View, supervising the tying of their luggage to the top of the stage. A red-faced drummer pushed his way through the batwing doors of the saloon and came to an abrupt halt at the sight of the mounted escort. His voice a high squeak, he asked, "Any problems, Marshal?"

"Nothing to worry about. Just a nice afternoon for a ride."

"My card, Marshal. I'm Sam Pallick. I get around some selling notions, whatnots. Just this day in the saloon, I saw . . . was sure I did . . ." He pulled in close, his voice died to a whisper. "Vince Whitney. He rode out of here not more'n a half hour ago. He's wanted in Eastern Colorado. Little town of Limon. Bank job. There was three hundred dollars on his head. Times being what they are, I could use a split a that."

High on a ridge above town, Wagner watched the stage and its outriders leave down the Ridge Road. A feeling of tiredness and resignation settled over him as he turned his horse toward the Rocking R.

Three miles out, Reuben and Tap pulled off the road, let the stage rumble by, made sure no one followed.

"Those girls have stirred a memory, Tap. One day when Albert Vale and I were about twelve, I helped him saw some wood and split it. Lunch time came, and Mrs. Vale fed us a roast beef sandwich and some of her homemade pickles. It was a hot day that had dawned warm and gathered heat about itself. She released us from our afternoon task. 'It's too hot, boys. Swimming weather, I'd say. Better save the rest of the woodpile for tomorrow.'

"We decided to go fishing, which usually led to getting wet anyway. As chance would have it, two of the girls that worked the Dixie Queen thought it was too hot to be trapped inside, so they sneaked out of their rooms to cool off in the river. Albert and I had just made our way there with fishing poles and a good supply of grasshoppers, had barely settled ourselves when we heard giggling. Curious, we gathered up our gear and hid behind a screen of willows, crouched there quiet-like and waited. We should have left when we first heard the girls, and since we didn't, we were trapped. Any noise on our part could lead to discovery, and if any word got back home, we'd get the razor strap. It was suddenly clear why mother had made this part of town and the greatest fishing hole around off limits.

"At first, the girls sat on the rocks and dangled their feet in the water, but pretty soon they were taking off clothes. Albert wanted to sneak away, but we didn't. It was like living in a nightmare, we couldn't have moved if we tried.

"Pretty soon there were voices from upriver. The girls grabbed up their clothes and slipped through the willows into the back door of the Dixie Queen. Albert and I kept to the brush, moved downstream, and fished that hole by Maria's café."

"I'd say you were lucky. I lived over Tonopah way. Hardly enough water for the bathtub. No fishing, no bathing girls, no matter what kind. Right now I'd settle for Maria's café and that pie and coffee you offered."

5

A pair of weeks passed, then one morning Wagner had the crew mending fence along Grizzly Creek when he saw Bonnie Picket gathering willow shoots. All thoughts of Candy were swept away.

Wagner had first seen the Picket woman at a country social. He had tried to get her to dance with him, but she twice turned him down. He'd forgotten that. What he knew was that she was a pretty woman and women found him charming. He'd just turn on the charm. Besides, here she was this day, a young widow well within the boundaries of the Rocking R. So as he saw it, she had practically come to him. Good enough. It stood to reason that an Indian woman used to white ways and a widow now would be ripe for a man, and Wagner figured that he'd be that man. All he had to do was apply his charm.

The next morning, he sent the Rocking R fencing crew far away from the creek so he could have the place to himself and hope for Picket's return.

Once the crew was well out of the way, he dressed for town. Peering into the murky bunkhouse mirror, he chuckled. Other men failed with the women because they didn't have his dash. He straightened his kerchief and the collar on his bright red shirt, gave his sidearm a jiggle, and strode outside to his horse.

High on a ridge half a mile from the creek, he broke out his pocket glass and waited for the Picket woman to appear. It had been a restless night for him. He'd tossed in his bunk and fought with the covers. When he did get to sleep, there were frustrating dreams. He was at a dance; the Picket woman was there. He asked for a dance and she refused. Asked again. Same answer. Today, he vowed, would be different. Today he'd get up close and personal. No more dreaming. No more refusals.

Midmorning found him still waiting. *Where the hell is she?* He'd overdressed, and a morning that had started out blustery was now warm, and except for thunderclouds building over the distant Old Woman Mountains to the west, gray skies had given away to blue. He was hot and uncomfortable and questioning the wisdom of his plan when she appeared.

Bonnie Pickett worked with practiced speed gathering willows to weave into baskets. She was hurrying to finish her task before the day got too warm. Outside of the occasional sale of chicken eggs, baskets that she weaved and sold were her sole means of support. Gunnison at the mercantile had just ordered five large laundry baskets, and it would take all the willow wands she could find to complete the order.

Whether it was concentration on her task or the splash and murmur of the creek, Bonnie was unaware of Wagner's presence until she heard the creak of leather as he dismounted. She turned to flee but was too late to evade him. Two steps and he had both of her wrists in his grip. The stubby kitchen knife she used to cut willows had dropped uselessly to the ground. He kicked it away from them.

"Mrs. Pickett, ma'am. Haven't seen much of you since your husband died. I've been meaning to call, but there's no need now you being here on Rocking R land and all."

"Let me go, Wagner."

"No hurry for that, ma'am. Surely no hurry. You and me both being unmarried and you riding practically to my door. No reason we shouldn't get better acquainted. We could have that dance I asked you for."

"I told you no before. The answer is still no."

He ignored her twisting attempts to break free. "Surely," he persisted, "you and me both being unattached and all." He pulled her closer.

Just downstream of the struggling pair was Bonnie's thirteen-year-old son, Billy. He had been loading willow shoots into two large baskets on their horse and had stopped momentarily to search the pool before him for the flash of small trout.

He had returned to the task of gathering willows when he caught the sound of voices upstream. He stood still. There it was again. It was his mother, and she was arguing with someone. He dropped the willows and reached to the scabbard for their shotgun.

Billy eased up the bank toward the voices. Through the screening willows he saw a large black mare with a white face blaze. It was ground reined on the opposite bank. On that same bank, a tall man in jeans and a gaudy red shirt was wrestling with his mother. It was the gunfighter Wagner, and he was armed with his pearl-handled revolver. Wagner was holding his mother by the wrists and keeping himself far enough away from her to avoid her kicks.

Clearly, Wagner was enjoying himself. "How about a little kiss?" he asked. "What could it hurt?"

It was obvious to Billy that he had to act, but fear gripped him. He had to stop the shaking. He searched for a tree limb to rest the gun on, one that would allow a clear shot at Wagner and would serve to steady the gun.

His mother twisted and got one wrist free. Wagner grabbed it back again wrenching her arm. Pain shot up to her shoulder.

"Damn you, Wagner. I said no."

"No? You're cussed uppity for an injun."

Catching a glimpse of her son on the opposite bank, she maneuvered Wagner to keep his back to the stream and to Billy. Ignoring her kicks, Wagner pulled her closer, slid a hand inside her buckskin jacket and bent in close to kiss her.

One hand loose again, she broke free, her face red with rage. He lunged to grab her, but she sidestepped him and rolled toward the stream, offering Billy a clear view of Wagner. All hesitation gone, Billy jumped clear of the brush that hid him. He was a mere thirty feet from the man. "Hold it right there, mister." Anger had rid him of his shakes. He had the shotgun trained dead level with Wagner's chest. Surprised at the edge of authority in his voice, he added, "Not another step."

No need. At the sight of the twin barrels, Wagner had come to a dead stop. Billy adjusted his aim to a point just below Wagner's belt. His hands were steady, his finger on the first trigger.

Bonnie waded the creek. Knee-deep on the far side, she stopped. Her trousers and buckskin jacket were muddy down one side, and her long black hair was splattered with mud. From there she addressed the Rocking R foreman. "Wagner, unbuckle your gun belt and drop it. Slowly and be awful careful. That shotgun has an uncertain trigger. Slowly now." Wagner had frozen in place. Bonnie waited another moment and added, "Don't you make a killer out of my boy."

Wagner stared across the creek. The twin holes of the ten gauge stared back at him. No matter how he calculated it, there could be little chance of a misfire and, at thirty feet, little chance the boy would miss. He swore at the pair of them. All the fun had gone out of the morning. Added to that, a boy had the drop on him, and it rankled. Grown men, wary of Wagner's reputation as a gunfighter, cowered like beaten dogs, turned yellow, and fled from him. But here he was this morning, helpless before a boy.

Time stretched out. The murmur of the creek, the whir of grasshoppers sounded unnaturally loud. Wagner toyed with the idea of rolling to the side and firing as he fell. The boy might hesitate. If he did, Wagner would win. But if the boy did not waver . . .

There entered in Wagner's mind the picture of his young friend, Proctor Biggs, writhing briefly in the dust of a Colorado cow town. He and Proctor had botched the bank job and a deputy's shotgun had cut Proctor nearly in half. There was a hole in Proctor's back big enough to put your two fists in. A glistening pool of blood darkened the street. Wagner had put his back to the deputy and fled, spurring his horse the length of the little town's Main Street. Several agonizing hours of riding later, he found a small town doctor willing to pry buckshot from his shoulder.

Across the creek, twin barrels awaited him. He carefully lowered his hands to his belt and let the gun and holster slide to the ground. He knew full well that this did not solve his problem, only put it off. If this story got out, his reputation as a gunfighter would be in question. He didn't think the woman would spread the story, but he couldn't free his mind of the boy. The boy was likely to tell anyone who'd listen. He made himself a promise that the boy would be silenced, but this was not the time to do it nor the way to do it.

He pointed a shaky finger at them. "You two keep off the Rocking R, or I'll have you shot for trespass." He spluttered to a stop, then added, "Comes to that, I'll do it myself."

Bonnie climbed up the slippery bank to Billy's side. "We'll be leaving soon enough. Now step away from that gun."

◅ LAWMAN'S DILEMMA ≻

He hesitated again, trying to find a way out of the situation. "You'd best hurry," she added. "You're making Billy nervous."

There is something to that, he thought. Dragging things out might not serve. The boy couldn't be as cool inside as he appeared, and fear was an unknown. The boy might panic at any time. He stepped away from the gun belt.

"That's it," Bonnie encouraged. "Now off with those boots and those britches."

Wagner was indignant. "Now see here, you got no right . . ."

"You got it wrong, Wagner. You've got no rights. Not when Billy's got the drop on you. You were so anxious to get those britches off, here's your chance."

Billy raised the shotgun to cover Wagner's head and shoulders. Wagner's fury continued, but he wasn't a fool. The twin holes of the ten gauge looked the size of drainpipes. The boy's eyes and hands remained rock steady. He had grit.

Bonnie climbed out of the stream and took over control of the shotgun. Her voice cut through the uneasy silence. "Now you've got me to deal with. When it comes to pulling the trigger on you, I've got no reluctance. Pitch those britches into the creek. We've got to fix it so that you can't follow us for a while." Twin muzzles followed him. He pulled off his boots and pants and dropped them in a grassy spot at the edge of the pool.

Bonnie was on one knee, the shotgun centered on his chest. "Billy, bring the horse up, and you, Wagner, pitch those britches in the creek." Once again her voice was high and clear, unrelenting.

Wagner did as he was ordered, but he had his say now. In a voice loaded with anger, he squeezed out, "I ain't gonna forget this . . . not never."

"Shy a couple of rocks at his horse, Billy." The first rock did it. The big horse angled off across the meadow dragging its reins. "By the time you get your britches on and catch your horse, we'll be long gone. Just remember the answer is no. No, I won't be your woman. You brought this whole thing down on yourself. And if somehow you get to thinking on revenge, if you get that feeling, keep in mind I was born and raised Indian."

Deciding to catch the horse before it wandered farther, Wagner began his trek across the meadow, and the incident turned bizarre. The sight of his lanky legs clad in long johns and socks got the most of Bonnie. Her rich laughter filled the meadow and stung Wagner to the center of his being.

Before he could catch his horse, they had doubled up on the gray and ridden out of sight.

6

Pan Sho's laundry sat halfway between Elder Creek's Main Street and the river and two hundred yards upriver from Gunnison's Mercantile. Starting from an abandoned cabin fashioned out of cottonwood logs, Pan Sho had added a large room on the side facing the river. There he housed washtubs and indoor drying lines. When time and money permitted, he built a cistern on a little rock ledge just above the laundry. Though he had to laboriously fill the cistern with buckets of water carried up from the river each night, he had as a result the luxury of running water inside his establishment.

Two years back he had come to Elder Creek dragging a handcart that contained a small woodstove, a pair of galvanized washtubs, and a meager pile of personal belongings. The sixteen miles of mostly uphill road from Silvercrown was a feat of endurance and a measure of his character. Within days of his arrival, he was settled and had erected a sign that proudly proclaimed Pan Sho Laundry in English and in Chinese.

For the first week or so, children and dogs pestered him as he made his rounds about town, but soon enough that ceased, and months passed by without incident. Pan Sho had been accepted into town. Then one warm evening in May, a pair of brothers, John and Edwin Weylyns, walking home late from the Odd Fellows Lodge, saw flames coming from Pan Sho's place. Yelling out an alarm, they ran toward the fire. A pinto and a small black horse were tied outside. Rearing and pulling at the reins, the horses were desperate to escape the fire. As the Weylyns drew nearer, two figures emerged from the laundry and galloped away on the horses.

The brothers hurried into the laundry. Following his cries for help, they burst through the smoke and flames and found Pan Sho tied to his bedstead. The brothers grabbed a tub of wash water and dumped it over Pan Sho, wetting him thoroughly.

Once Pan Sho was free and out of the smoke-filled building, they poured water from another tub right onto the fire. More help came, and a bucket brigade worked from the river to the fire.

Although the damage was limited to a hole in the floor and one scorched wall, everyone present knew they had come close to losing a laundry and a hard-working citizen.

When Reuben Braddock arrived at the scene, the fire was out. He addressed the Weylyns, "Was anyone in that fire?"

John answered, "It's Pan Sho's laundry. Edwin and I found him in there tortured and tied to his bed. Wood slivers shoved under his fingernails. They believed he had money squirreled away. He wouldn't tell them anything. Then, I guess they decided to burn him out, shut him up. We hurried him to Doc Miller's place. Except for his fingers, he ain't burned bad."

"What about his fingers?"

"You'll need to see him, see the fingers."

Reuben sensed a reluctance to describe Pan Sho's hands. "You think he knows who did it?"

John answered, "Oh, he knows them all right. He thinks they planned to kill him, so they didn't try to hide their faces."

"Could be they heard you shouting out the fire alarm. That far off Main Street they figured they'd get away clean. Didn't even bother to hide their horses. I'll go see Pan Sho."

Reuben pounded up the stairs to Doc Miller's office. Miller turned from his work as Reuben entered the office. "I'm glad to see you, Braddock. Before I cover his hands, I want you to look at them." He held up Pan Sho's right hand. It was blackened and bloody. Two of the nails were torn out, the ends of the fingers split where burning slivers of wood had been forced under the nails.

Pan Sho was conscious, his jaw set tight. Reuben looked into the man's eyes, saw the pain etched there, and saw too the stubbornness and determination that had brought the man this far. He understood the effort Pan Sho was exerting to keep from crying out. "Pan Sho, the Weylyns say you know the men."

"Yes, I know them. Mr. Barnes. Mr. Olsen. I worked late. It was dark when I fill cistern from river. Inside they wait for me. They say if I pay money I will have no fire. How can they stop me from fire? Last week I told them no. They said, 'You will have very bad fire.' I said no, no fire. Now I know. They want Pan Sho's money." He struggled for self-control. "See my hand? When will I work? When will I buy food?"

"We will make sure you have food, Pan Sho." He looked again at the man's hands. "I'll get the men who did this. You have my word on it."

After his talk with Pan Sho and the Weylyns, Braddock strode down to the Mountain View saloon. A broad splash of yellowish light from under the batwing doors spilled onto the boardwalk. Someone was giving the tinny piano a workout. The poker table was busy; a thin blue smear of tobacco smoke hung in the air just above the lamp shades. It appeared to be business as usual in the Mountain View.

Braddock stood a moment just outside the door, letting his eyes adjust to the glare and banking his anger. He checked the rounds in his .44 and slid the gun back into its holster. After seeing Pan Sho's hands, he wanted to hurt the men who had done it, wanted to step on their hands, grind them into the floor, choke them until they turned gray and fell lifeless. He could do neither. It was one of the problems that came with the badge.

Keeping his hands free, he shouldered his way through the batwing doors and strode to the middle of the saloon where he stopped and quietly surveyed the customers. The piano went silent. Sonny, behind the bar, stopped mopping at its surface and looked up expectantly.

Braddock took his time, making a mental record of those present.

A quarter turn put him a few steps behind the pair Pan Sho had named. They were quiet and hunched over their beer. Reuben addressed the bartender. "Say, Sonny, do you know who might own a small black horse and a pinto? They're both saddled but wandering off toward the river."

At the mention of loose horses, Barnes, the skinny one, stood up. His partner, a bleary-eyed saloon regular, grabbed his arm and pulled him back down to the barstool, but the damage had been done. Braddock stepped closer, the acrid smell of burning cloth clung to the pair of them. Seemingly without moving, Braddock filled his hand with his .44 Colt.

The click of poker chips from the card table ceased. A deeper silence fell over the saloon. "Gently now, you boys put both hands on the bar top. Spread 'em out where I can see 'em." He stared. Barnes had blood under his nails. They must have come straight from the fire hoping to blend in. How could they sit there drinking with a man's blood on their hands? He resisted the urge to pistol-whip them where they sat. Instead, he disarmed them, sliding their pistols down the bar to the bartender. "Put those guns behind the bar and give me a hand, will ya, Sonny?" With his left hand, he pulled handcuffs from his jacket pocket.

Once the men were frisked and secured, with a nod of thanks to Sonny, he marched them out the swinging doors. There at the hitching rack stood the pinto and the black.

"Marshal," declared an indignant Olsen, "What's the idea? There's them horses, and they ain't wandered nowhere."

"Why, that is a fact. Seems I was mistaken. We are, all the same, going to just keep walkin'. There's been a fire, and you were seen leaving it."

They continued up the boardwalk to where it ended just past the Little Willow Hotel. There they took to the dusty street and stopped in the near dark by a cluster of men. Two of the men held kerosene lanterns that provided a dull gleam and cast long shadows into the street. They were talking about the fire.

Braddock addressed the gathering. "Anyone recognize these men?"

Edwin raised his lantern and allowed its light to fall on the faces of Braddock's prisoners. "Yes," he said, "I've seen them at the saloon. And saw them tonight."

"Where did you see them tonight?"

"We saw their faces in the light from the fire at Pan Sho's."

"They were at the fire?"

"Yes. We saw them leaving it. Saw their horses too. Like I told you before, there was a pinto and that little black mare that Olsen rides."

"John, is that so? There was light enough to see all that?"

"Plenty of light, Marshal. It was them, no doubt."

The bleary-eyed man was in a panic. "God sakes, Marshal. He's just a Chinaman."

"Yes, and I'm just a marshal, and you're just a barfly."

The skinny man spoke up, "Other places I been, they don't count it no crime, burnin' out Chinee."

"You must be in the wrong place then. This is Elder Creek, and there's a clear call for justice here. Pity you didn't hear it. I'm charging the pair of you with arson and attempted murder. In the morning I'll be moving you to Silvercrown for trial." He hesitated, his disgust building to a dangerous level. "And I'm telling you straight out, if you give me any trouble on the trail, any excuse at all, I'll surely shoot the pair of you. You're the most disgusting, wrong-headed bums I've ever heard of."

Braddock turned and addressed the crowd. "As for the rest of you, feel proud that you stepped forward. You made quick work of the fire, saved a man's life. There's no doubt there. You could've walked on by, gone home, and closed your doors. Left Pan Sho to burn. But you didn't. That takes the play away from bums like this." He paused looking at each of them, remembering them. "It makes a town worth living in."

7

Two days after the fire at Pan Sho's place, Maria waited in her café for Reuben's return from Silvercrown. She was washing dishes and glancing occasionally out of her tiny kitchen window at the Ridge Road

Bonnie broke the silence. "Maria, you've been watching the road to Silvercrown most of the morning. Chances are you'll wear it out."

"It'll be ore wagons that wear it out. But if my luck holds, Marshal Reuben Braddock will arrive by that road this very afternoon."

"That was my guess," said Bonnie. "And it might explain the bath and the fresh dress."

"And a little rose water. It all helps. Short, round, and Mexican is what I am." She sighed, looking at her friend. "Not slender and pretty like you. Every man in town has eyes for you, Bonnie."

Bonnie's face darkened at the memory of the incident with Wagner at Grizzly Creek. "Be happy with what you are, Maria. Besides, you've got the marshal. That big man comes near you and you melt. He melts. It's like you two were courting."

It sounded like an accusation. Maria turned and looked a question at her. Bonnie responded with a shrug. "Could be I'm jealous. All I get is sneaky looks and bad offers."

Maria's face grew flushed at the thought of Reuben's last visit. "You shoulda seen him, Bonnie. Three days back. He came riding into town tall in the saddle like a hero out of a picture book. I was expecting him, bathed, washed my hair. Wore my red dress. He likes the smell of my hair when I use rose water."

"Yes, you said that."

"Um, I suppose. Up to then we were just friends." She paused, her face flushed again.

Bonnie waited for Maria to go on. When she didn't, Bonnie turned toward her with impatience. "Yes, Maria? Up till then you were just friends? You can't leave me with half a story."

Maria dried her hands, took a quick look at the Ridge Road, and sat down with her friend at the window overlooking Main Street. "When he was through at the livery, he crossed the street to my place, stood on the porch, and pounded the dust from his clothes with his big hat. Then just like always, he took his favorite seat overlooking the street, the one I'm in right now. He plopped down a silver dollar and said, 'Bring me beer and steak until this is all gone.' He always said that. Somewhere that morning he'd put on a clean shirt, shaved. My handsome *Jefe*.

"I went to the door, bolted it, and said, 'So you won't be disturbed.' Of course, I meant we will not."

"Maria! You waylaid him!"

"Not like you might think. I had no plans. I just didn't want to share him. Anyway, this last time he hung up his hat and gun belt and came into the kitchen to talk to me while I cooked. He was standing directly behind me, and my body . . . I swear sometimes the body gets loose and acts on its own . . . My body sagged back into him. He grabbed my shoulders to steady me, and for a long minute we just stood that way. Pretty soon he was rubbing my arms, kissing my neck. He was whispering so softly into my ear that I strained to hear him. By then I was shaking so. I turned into him, reached up like a dance hall hussy, and kissed him."

She left the table and returned to the kitchen window to get a view of the Ridge Road. She let the silence stretch out, then said, "Those big hands . . . so gentle. Right here in my little kitchen."

8

With Barnes and Olsen cached in the root cellar jail for the night, Braddock called on Tap Trundle, Elder Creek's blacksmith and mayor. The night had turned cool. They hunched over the coals in Tap's forge and sipped old coffee. "Sorry about the coffee, Reuben. I answered the fire call and come pretty near ruining this batch."

"I'm grateful for it but most grateful you were here to answer that fire call. I was just approaching town when I smelled the smoke. I'd been out settling a dispute at the Jumping J. As there wasn't much to the dispute, I might as well have stayed in town." Braddock went quiet for a few moments, staring into the coals of the forge. Tap waited. Considering the fact that Braddock had only been in town a pair of weeks, the two men were as comfortable together as old friends. "Tap, I'm following up on something I was told. Seems that more than a few of the men that hang out at the Mountain View are firebugs. I'm told that they visit people in the middle of the night wearing masks. They break right into a house and tell them to pay 'insurance money' or risk a fire."

"That's just it, Reuben. They sell fire insurance. If you don't pay up, you have a fire."

"That's extortion. Big city stuff."

"I guess it'd work anywhere. It's affecting everybody, and it's got worse since the Golden Rooster fire. Todd Farkin had built the Rooster mostly with his own hands. Had it just about ready to open when he got a visit from Barnes and Olsen. He said he considered paying them just to hold them off until he could get help. But he was short of funds. He talked with me and a few other people. We set up patrols and was out the night the Rooster burned, but unfortunately, we chased a decoy fire down by Maria's. By the time we got back here, the Golden Rooster was too far gone to save. They'd burned him out.

"A few nights later, three men visited me. Kicked my door in. Two held a pistol on me while the other one read me the terms. I think another man was outside on watch. Nothing I could do then. They had kerchiefs over their face, but I was pretty sure the man reading me the terms was Pelham, the blackjack and poker dealer from the Mountain View. I held them off that night with promises, but in the end I refused to pay. A few nights later, two men came around to burn me out. I caught them at it.

"I knocked one of them flying. The other one skinned out the door before I could get a hold of him. My forge was still going. I tied that cuss to my anvil and worked the bellows awhile. The coals got so hot they heated every corner of the shop. I took my time, let him sweat, if you see what I mean. I put an iron in the forge until it was white-hot and held it close enough to his face to singe his beard. He made me a bunch of promises. I didn't say a darned thing but put the iron back in the forge. We both watched while it got white-hot again. More promises, wheedling. Never saw a man break down like that. Told him to leave town and if I saw him again, I'd brand his forehead. Nobody's been back bothering me about 'fire insurance,' and I don't see that one around at all. Must have left town."

Reuben hesitated before commenting. The picture of Pan Sho's hands had come to him. Torture was revolting to him, yet this man had threatened to use it. Tap meant well. No question there, but it was wrong.

Tap waited for a reply. It was slow in coming. He sensed that he'd struck a wrong chord somewhere. Reuben looked over at him, the light from the forge flickering across the man's strong features. "You tell me, Tap. You saw Pan Sho's hands. That seem right to you?"

Tap had great respect for this man and would do about anything he'd ask. He wanted to be on his good side and now, almost without thinking about it, had alienated him. Maybe not alienated but had struck a jarring note. "Maybe I shouldn't have threatened him with torture, but I got action. He's flat left town. Left the country. So it worked."

"I see that, Tap, and I'd agree that we need to rid ourselves of that outfit, but if we are no better than they are, if we blur the line between the law and the lawless, we begin to resemble the enemy, and that doesn't serve our ends. The law seems slow and cumbersome sometimes, and that makes it awful tempting to move ahead on our own, but we can't do that. Can't. Not and claim to be civilized."

"I didn't have law to go to, Reuben."

Reuben nodded in agreement. "That's so, but if you catch somebody like that again, you turn him over to me. I don't agree with torture, but I can sure hold 'em for trial. We'll work together, whittle away at that outfit until there's nothing left of it. I think quite a few people are paying protection. There is enough of it going on to put people out of business. Meanwhile, it keeps that gang alive. Town can't afford it. And it's dangerous. If one of their fires got going in the wrong place, the whole town would go up in smoke."

"Putting away Barnes and Olsen was a good start, Reuben, but what worries me is that even if the gang loses a man or two, more show up. And the gang hangs out at the Mountain View looking like miners, cowhands, teamsters, and whatnot. They blend in, and I'm not sure how many there are. And the money, there may be big money involved, maybe bigger than we imagine. They've even threatened to go after the ore wagons."

"Are you sayin' the mine pays them too?"

"Could be. There's been no trouble at the mine for a year or so. As for help on this, you might have a talk with Sonny. He'd just as soon the gang was gone. Be sure of one thing, Reuben. You can count on my help. I'd like to get things back to where the only crime in town is the grub they serve at the Mountain View."

9

Bonnie walked out the back door of Maria's café to take the laundry from the clothesline. She stopped on the back steps for a moment shielding her eyes from the sun. There was movement at the back of the woodshed. Cautiously, worrying that it might be Wagner come to torment them, she covered half the distance to the shed and stopped. It wasn't Wagner; it was her son, Billy. He had a saddle on their desert-bred gray and was tying on a bedroll. She dropped her basket and ran to him. He was agitated and as near panic as she had ever seen him. "Billy, What is it?"

"It's Wagner. I seen him do it." He pointed up river. "Tad White was with me and we were fishing the river just down here. Back of Maria's. We saw a carriage going fast, those black horses were flying along the river road and approaching the bridge. Then, up on the bridge, somebody jumped up and waved a blanket. We saw the horses and all go off the other side. Then we saw someone come off the bridge, sneak down through the willows, and go into the back of the saloon."

"How do you figure it was Wagner?"

"We ran up there a ways. Got close enough to see him clear and clean. But I gotta hurry, Mom. Holmes came over from the livery. He says that Jimmy Hodges was killed in that wreck and Wagner is telling everyone that I done it. He's working up a crowd, and they'll be riding soon."

"You just hold tight. We'll tell Marshal Braddock about it."

"He's here?"

A silence followed. Finally, Bonnie shook her head. "Maria says he'll probably be here this afternoon."

He gave the saddle cinch an extra yank and let the stirrup down. He looked up at her. "That'll be too late, Mom. Wagner wants me dead. He's afraid I'll tell about Grizzly Creek, get people laughing at him."

"That's crazy."

"Maybe, or maybe he's crazy. But it doesn't matter. I've got to go. They'll be riding soon."

Bonnie knew who they were and knew Billy was right. She made up her mind. "You fill canteens. I'll get some food from Maria. Go up desert to Yancey's. You'll be safe there, and I'll know where you are." She was holding him, brushing absently at his hair. "Stay out of sight. Travel steady."

"I know. Don't push the horse. Don't skyline yourself. Travel when it's cool."

Minutes later she came back with a package of jerky and tortillas. Billy gave her a hug and vaulted into the saddle. He looked down at her, tears streaming. "Don't forget me, Ma." He dug his heels in. He and the gray disappeared into the trees. Long after he was out of sight, she stood frozen to the spot, and half to herself, half aloud, she said, "Don't forget you? You are all I have. You and Maria."

After a long while, she returned to her laundry chore. She felt so helpless. Was this all she could do? See to the chores and worry? She knew that she should feel relieved that Billy had ridden away before he was found, but she felt only dread. He was young, too young for what he had to do. She felt the urge to call him back but knew she couldn't. Wagner had set things into motion that she couldn't control. "Take a lesson," her aunt had said, "from the willows along the river. In flood time they bend but do not break. When the water goes down, when the storm goes away, they will still be there. If we are like the willows, we will always be here."

10

With Barnes and Olsen safely in the county jail, Braddock left Silvercrown in a hurry, trailing their horses. An ornery-looking mess of clouds was building up from the southwest. It was going to dump a pile of rain somewhere, and he hoped to be under cover when it did. As a result, his only concession to breakfast was a handful of beef jerky and a firm promise of livery time for the horses.

Three hours later, with the storm safely off to the east, he pulled his little caravan into the cover of piñon a half hour from Elder Creek. From his vantage point, he could glass the town and much of the countryside.

Braddock dismounted and, despite the horse's wishes, tightened the saddle cinch and then for good measure tugged at his own belt. He had better luck with the horse. No matter how he tugged, his gun belt, loaded down with cartridges and a .44 Colt, defeated his efforts.

He looked down regretfully at a growing paunch. He knew the cause of it, of course. All he had to do was eat less at Maria's café and spend more time walking. There wasn't much chance he would do either.

Just an inch shy of six foot, Reuben was broad through the shoulders and thick in the arms and chest. His dark-brown hair had a sprinkling of gray at the temples. He was a man who sat a horse easily and spent many hours there. On the ground he was deceptively quick with a light-footed swing to his walk. Riding and splitting wood kept his body taut.

Still, there was a paunch building. No question there.

He fished a spyglass out of his coat pocket and looked off left across the Sulfur Hills and the Jumping J spread into the Alvordo Desert with its salt sinks, alkali flats, and deserted mining claims. Parts of it were still roamed by a small band of Washoe Indians. Four days' ride to the north was Yancey's legendary Lazy Y.

The cattle ranches were peripheral, hanging to the edge of the desert. Silver claims, except for the Ketchum Mine operating out of the Bluestone Peaks, had all been abandoned, boarded up. With the prospectors gone, Braddock and the Washoe were the only souls who knew the Alvordo. For that reason, any travelers forced to cross the Alvordo stuck to the Military Road and the sure water of Morning Glory Wells.

Even now, the Alvordo's vast expanses, its stark and awful beauty pulled at him. "What do you say, little horse? We delivered our prisoners. Maybe we could take a few days, prospect a little. We could stay at my old camp under the Keller Rim."

He dug his finger into his pocket and pulled out a large nickel-plated watch tied to a slender buckskin fob. "Right now it's half past one, and I'm tired. Time to get you to the livery and me to Maria's. We'll both put on the feedbag, settle back. Take a nap."

He slipped the watch back into his pocket and spent a minute scanning the fifty or so houses that made up Elder Creek. They were mostly shacks, hot in the summer and, if you got six feet from a stove, bone cold in the winter. Still there weren't many places in Nevada that were any different, and when you got down to it, Elder Creek was home. And Elder Creek had Maria.

Before slipping the glass into its case, he swung it across the slope between her place and the river. He pictured an expanded garden there. Big as any in town and rich with carrots, cabbages, raspberries, apple trees. Rich as butter. Let somebody else keep law and order. He'd retire.

Right now, if he was at Maria's, there'd be cool beer and a steak with salsa hot enough to take the bluing off a gun barrel. He shook his head as if to clear it and turned to the horse. "I've been dreaming, big friend, and dreaming will get you killed." He tried to remember which old-timer had said that. It didn't matter. It was right; he'd been too casual, and there was something about the town that nagged him. He went back to the spyglass. In a moment he knew what had bothered him. It wasn't a matter of what was there: a fire, a gunfight, a mob. It involved what was not there. There were no people about in the gardens or on the street. Particularly, and most especially, there were no horses at the hitching rail in front of the Mountain View saloon.

He heaved himself into the saddle and set off at a ground-eating gallop. Gone were thoughts of a steak at Maria's. Sure as Saturday night sin, something was wrong in town.

11

If Braddock had been in town at midmorning, he'd have seen the peaceful place he hoped for. An early cloudiness that had obscured the sun and held Elder Creek for a time in its cool gave way before noon; the sun bathed the valley in early summer warmth. Doors and windows were opened. People were about in the streets or tending their gardens. They were using any excuse they could find to get outside.

But the peace wasn't to last. Shortly before noon, Vance Wagner rode in and tied up at the hitch rack beside Gunnison's mercantile. He was in a sour mood. This day there was whiskey on his breath and a ruddy flush to his thin face.

Just as he tied up, a pair of punchers appeared out of the mercantile. They were carrying two blocks of salt apiece, which they dumped into the back of the Rocking R wagon. Pat Beacher, the older of the two, jumped off the dock and fastened the tailgate.

Beacher was a short man somewhere in his forties with big scarred hands and heavy arms. His face was deeply grooved. His low-crowned gray hat was stained around the sweatband, its brim broken from constant creasing. He walked slightly stooped and looked very much like a saddened, worn leprechaun.

His partner, Whitey Krebs, jumped off the dock nearly falling into a graceless pile. He was a skinny white-haired kid dressed like a farmer in bib overalls and a too-large denim jacket buttoned only at the top. His straw hat sat low on his forehead. In his hip pocket he had jammed a well-worn pair of leather and canvas gloves.

Neither man carried a sidearm.

Harnessed to the Rocking R wagon were two chestnut mares matched for color and size. All-purpose horses, they were as much at home in the hay meadow or the woodlot as they were in town. They were Reno Rawlins's prizes and a statement: look prosperous, be prosperous. Tied next to them at the hitch rack was Beacher's hipshot pinto.

"Is that it?" queried Wagner, glaring at Beacher from the plank loading dock. He ignored Krebs.

Beacher, brushing salt from his pants, said, "That's it except for the flour and bacon. We can get that and be gone in two, three minutes."

Wagner was looking across the street at the livery stable where a pair of blacks were being hitched to a shiny carriage with a folded-down top. The horses were high-spirited and fidgety. The livery hand bustled about talking to them and getting things sorted out. Just inside the livery door where the sun failed to reach, a small figure in a gray suit was impatiently slapping his pants leg with a buggy whip.

Wagner addressed Beacher again. "Suppose I decide when you leave. You see anything of the Indian kid Pickett? I've got an urge to talk to him."

Krebs shrugged, and Beacher answered the foreman. "Guess we haven't." Wagner seemed to be waiting for more of an answer, so Beacher ended up with, "We'll sure keep our eyes open."

"You do that," replied Wagner. "You've got a pretty heavy load of wire and nails there. I'm guessing it'll take you a good two hours to get to the ranch. More. You better go into the Mountain View and order up lunch. Lunch and beer for the three of us."

With Wagner heading into the mercantile, Beacher pointed at the rolls of smooth wire that they'd loaded. "I wish they was a better wire. You make a fence out of this stuff, and you're making a place for cows to rub. You make a piece of drift fence, and two weeks later they've got it rubbed down."

Krebs agreed, "That fence we fixed yesterday was a piece we put in this spring. But how . . ." He looked from the wire to Beacher and back again.

"The how is I'd put stickers on it. Something sharp."

Wagner had come back onto the platform and heard the conversation. He towered over them.

"There you go, you old coot. Dreamin' ag'in. Maybe we should buy a bunch of spurs and take the rowels off. Tie those rowels on the wire. Ha-ha. Ain't you somethin'."

Beacher burned inwardly but held back a reply. Confronting Wagner could lead to another brawl, and he'd lost twice to the bigger man. He wouldn't put it above Wagner to start another fight right here in town. It would draw an audience and add to Wagner's reputation as a tough guy. Even if he beat Wagner this time, the owner had promised that one more brawl and someone was going to get fired. Since Reno Rawlins was afraid of the foreman's gun, Beacher would be the one that would get fired. He took comfort in the thought that someday Wagner would fall and fall hard. His kind usually did. Beacher vowed to be there when it happened.

Wagner broke into his reverie. "Well, you gonna go order lunch?"

Krebs fidgeted and looked at his partner. Beacher said, "We ain't got no money on us."

"Who asked ya? Rocking R will pay. You get goin'. I'll take care of the flour and bacon."

Wagner took another quick look at the livery stable and disappeared into the mercantile.

The kid seemed hesitant. Beacher looked at him and said, "You don't have to like him to eat lunch with him. It's done all the time. Me, I'm getting a plate of beef and beans and one of those pickled eggs they keep in a jar. And a beer. That's what he'll want, so I'll just order three of them. That all right?"

"It's all right, only I was thinking, if I'm goin' to be eating in town, I'd sooner it was at Maria's."

"Yeh, sure. And I suppose if you was getting ready for bed, you'd just as soon it was a feather bed in a grand hotel. I like Maria's. She turns out a berry cobbler that makes me homesick. But you can sooner all the sooners you want. It ain't what he offered."

The Mountain View was half full of idle men. Beacher took a stool at the end of the bar near the swinging doors, and Whitey joined him. Beacher patted the stool on his left. "You sit here. Wagner always takes the corner stool. He don't like nobody behind him."

"I noticed that. Don't you ever wonder about him? I mean, before he came here."

"I don't wonder nothin', and I expect you to learn to do the same."

Their plates were nearly empty before they were joined by Wagner. "Had to wait while they wrapped the bacon," he said. He drained his beer and waved his glass at the bartender. "Get me another, Sonny. And beer for the house."

The beer was met by a murmur of approval from the barflies. But Beacher declined. "Me and the kid have had enough. Besides, if I have two beers, I might fall off my horse."

Some of the barflies thought it wise to laugh at that. The burly barkeep scurried about filling glasses. Krebs used a piece of bread to mop at the bean juice and gravy at the bottom of his plate.

Beacher stared for the thirtieth time at the painting of a nearly nude woman that hung at the back of the bar. Wagner caught him at it. "Whatcha lookin' at, ya old coot? Do you suppose she's gonna come down here and give ya a big smooch?" More laughter.

Krebs shoved his plate back and stood up to go. Then, worrying that Beacher might think him presumptuous, he looked apologetically at his partner and sat back down.

"No, you were right. It's time to go."

Wagner, wary of giving away any amount of authority, looked up from cutting his steak and said, "Flour and bacon are in the wagon. You'd best get it back to the ranch."

Krebs and Beacher were halfway to the door when three shots rang out and then three more. They were all from upriver. Most of the saloon customers emptied into the street. Down it at a fast clip came two riders. The foremost was yelling, "There's a fancy carriage over the bridge. Went right off the side. Looks like the banker's rig."

Both riders slid to a halt between the mercantile and the tavern. The second rider, not to be left out of the excitement, added, "We seen it in the water as we came over the bridge. It's awful."

Wagner spoke up from the boardwalk. "You see the driver?"

"You can't tell. It's all churned up. Might be under the horses, under the carriage."

At that announcement, Wagner stepped forward and took charge. "Beacher, you fetch Doc Miller. Krebs, you get our wagon home. Use the ford downstream of the bridge if you have to. Rest of you ride with me."

And that is how, in the absence of Barnes and Olsen, Wagner took control of the Mountain View gang.

A few townspeople traipsed up to the bridge or stood around on street corners trying to learn what had happened, but when the gang rode, people disappeared into their houses, closed and locked their doors.

12

When Braddock rode in from Silvercrown, he found Elder Creek's streets were still empty. At the livery, he tried to raise Holmes but gave up. He guessed the man was grabbing a quick beer at the Mountain View. He settled the horses into stalls with oats and water and hurried across the street to Maria's. She'd know what had emptied the streets. He'd been there a scant minute when there was a pounding at the door. "Marshal, you in there?"

"Yeh. What do you want?"

"It's me, Garvey. That posse is back. They've gone into the saloon for a beer. Talk is that they'll be riding again soon. The banker's boy had a carriage wreck . . ."

Braddock yanked the door open. "What's that? A wreck, you say?"

"A carriage wreck. They say Billy Pickett caused it. Waved a blanket at the horses as they got to the bridge. They say his footprints are up there."

"Sounds like crap to me. Why would the boy do something like that?"

"The Blankenship boy says it was Billy. Says he seen it. People say Billy is jealous of the banker's boy . . . the carriage, horses, and all. Wagner's getting the posse ready to go back looking."

"Go back looking? If they've already been out, when did it happen?"

"It musta been about noon. Soon after that, the saloon bunch rode out to the Pickett place. Shot it up some, I heard. Didn't find nobody, so they rode back here."

"Damn those people! Why the hell didn't you come get me?"

"I just got to town, Reuben."

"Well, sure enough. So did I. When you say they are back here, you mean the Mountain View saloon. Am I right?"

"Yessir."

"Get me a fresh horse, Garvey. And that roan I like to ride. I'll trail it. We'll see to the posse as soon as you get back."

Back inside he was confronted by Maria and Bonnie. Maria was tugging at his shirt. "Where are you going, *Jefe*?"

"There's been a carriage wreck. They're blaming Billy. I've gotta find him, but first I gotta break up that damn mob."

"Marshal," Bonnie spoke up. "We know about the wreck and what Wagner is saying. I sent Billy off. We had to keep Wagner's mob away from him."

"You mean that he's run. Worst thing he could do, Bonnie. Makes him look guilty."

Maria was tugging at his shirt again. "You weren't here. That Mountain View bunch was riding the streets just like they did before you came to be our marshal. They want to hang Billy. No trial. No nothing. Holmes came to warn Billy. I'm hiding Holmes in my root cellar till dark. Don't you see, Reuben? Billy had to go."

Bonnie broke down; tears welled up and spilled over. She brushed at them with her apron corner. "He can't get a fair deal in this town. Not when you're gone."

Maria was crying too. They were tears of anger and frustration. "The town has mostly good people," she said, "but they close their doors, and that bunch at the saloon runs things. And now they've got Wagner to lead them. He's a very angry man. Twice I've had to hide Billy and his mom. Wagner has been lookin' for 'em. Once he said Billy stole a horse. Now this wreck. Bonnie and the boy have been with me since yesterday late. They were here today when news of the wreck came down the street."

Braddock was a shade relieved. "So Billy couldn't have been at the bridge and caused the wreck. Why didn't you tell me this when I first came in?"

"First thing you did when you got here was sweep me off my feet. Garvey was right behind you. Neither of you gave me a chance."

"Guess we didn't. Just the same, I've got to bring that boy in."

Bonnie broke in then, saying, "Billy and Tad White were fishing in the river just off Maria's garden. They saw a man at the bridge. Saw him leap up waving a blanket or a shirt. They think he was lying on the bridge waiting for the carriage. The horses shied and spilled over the other side and into the river. He used the cover of the willows to come back downriver and into the back of the saloon. The boys sneaked up along the willows to see who it was. Wagner was the man. They saw him 'clear and clean' when they got closer. That's what Billy said."

"Let Billy go, *Jefe*. Please." It was Maria tugging at his shirt again.

"I can't," he said. He looked at both women, stroked Maria's arms absently for a moment, then turned to go out the door. He stopped then and turned back to them. "Suppose I let him go. He'll just keep on running. All his life he'll be lookin' back over his shoulder. Every stranger he sees could be a lawman or a bounty hunter. I've seen it all before. Seen it ruin lives. To avoid that, I'll bring him in, and we'll clear him. Meanwhile, just don't mention Tad White's name to anyone. Holmes either."

Bonnie broke in, "No posse?"

"No, ma'm, no posse. I'll bring him in by myself, safe and sound. That's a promise. How long ago did you send him to the Jumping J?"

"He's been gone about three hours. I sent him up desert."

"Up? To Yancey's?"

Bonnie nodded.

"Across all that damn desert?"

"Yes, Marshal. Across all that damn desert." Bonnie had her back up. "He's not a child, and he's safer there than he is here."

"For the time being, that's true. I gotta ask some questions uptown, get a fresh horse, and break up Wagner's posse.

Maria, fix me a little grub. Please. And, Bonnie, what was Billy wearing?"

"He's wearing blue overalls, faded and getting a little short for him now. And a blue shirt, a buckskin jacket that belonged to his father . . . still way big for him . . . high-top work shoes." As calmly as she could through her tears, Bonnie added, "I'd have gone with him, but there was no time to get a second horse. Couldn't go to the livery anyway. I figured that Wagner had a man hidden there. We've just got that one horse, a little desert—bred gray, and we didn't steal a horse from no one, especially not that damn . . . excuse me . . ." She bit her tongue and held back what she had in mind, then went on, "Gunslinger, Wagner."

"Wagner again?"

"Yes, Wagner. Two days back he caught me working on the creek and assaulted me. There's no telling what would have happened, but Billy grabbed our shotgun and trained it on him. Stopped him cold. That's why he's after Billy, and it's what the posse is all about. I'm guessin' he can't swallow the fact that Billy got the drop on him."

"All right, Bonnie. I can't break up that damn posse standin' here."

Maria hustled in from the kitchen with two small packages. "Tortillas and a piece of ham, *Jefe*. Some cheese . . . jerky. You will be careful?"

At the door he turned, slid a package into each pocket of his great coat, and took Maria's hands in his. Ignoring Bonnie's presence, he said, "I was hoping this afternoon."

She looked into his eyes. "That's me too, Reuben. When you get back."

"*Si*. When I get back. Garvey's here. Gotta go." He took her in his arms and kissed her once, lightly on the lips. It was almost a ghost of a kiss. "I'll be back. Soon as I can."

Maria locked the door behind him and collapsed into the nearest chair. Bonnie came to console her. Maria said, "I've been getting a vision, Bonnie. A waking nightmare you could say. In it I see two figures battling. It tells me that somewhere in an alley or somewhere on a lonely trail, Reuben will come face-to-face with that damn Wagner. When he does, one of them will die. Of this I'm certain." She looked up at Bonnie. "I have great respect for Reuben and for what he does, but I could love him without that damn badge. Of this I am also certain."

13

While Reuben stored food into saddlebags, tied on his great coat, and checked the horse's cinch strap, he questioned Garvey. "Can you make heads or tails of that carriage wreck?"

"Like I said, the Blankenship boy saw somebody jump out of the bushes and wave a blanket at the horses just as they were getting to the bridge. He says it was Billy Pickett."

"Where was this blanket waver?"

"He says Billy was in the bushes at the north side of the bridge."

"And the horses went off the south side?"

"Why no, Reuben. They went off the north side."

"North side? So you tell me, Garvey, why the hell would the horses shy toward what frightened them?"

Garvey looked at Reuben like a door had opened. "Why, they wouldn't. Would they?"

"Wouldn't is right. That boy is lying. Looks like Billy's got more than one enemy in this town. We'll get him back here and clear him, and we'll nail the coward who actually caused this wreck.

"Bear with me just a moment, Garvey. I need to check the back of the café for the gray's hoofprint. I wanta know it when I see it again."

Braddock and Garvey, their horses in tow, found a crowd gathered in front of the Mountain View saloon. Vance Wagner was just finishing a speech. "We've found a home here, all of us, and we can't have murderers and horse thieves runnin' loose. And this Pickett, horse crazy like all Indians, is a horse thief and a killer. He stole a Rocking R horse, and now he's so jealous of the banker's boy and that matched pair of blacks that he killed 'em. Killed the boy! Killed the horses! Killed 'em all!"

Wagner was working the crowd like a veteran politician, and they were responding. "I say we string him up!" With that, Wagner made his way off the boardwalk and to his horse.

Braddock challenged him. "What's this? Vance Wagner, you in charge of this outfit?"

His hand on the saddle horn, Wagner turned and addressed Braddock. "Just a citizen's group, Marshal. We're ready to ride after that killer."

"Why, who would that be?"

"Billy Pickett. He run those horses off the bridge. Killed the banker's boy, and seeing that you weren't in town . . ." There was a murmur of approval from the crowd.

"You're wrong, Wagner. At the time of the wreck, the boy was nowhere near that bridge."

"The Blankenship boy saw him."

"Says he did." Braddock addressed the crowd then. "This man is lying to you. Things just didn't happen the way you been told. You've just got to be patient. We'll get the whole story when I bring Billy back."

A voice from the back of the crowd yelled out, "We don't need to wait. We know the killer, and we've got a rope. We'll just find him and get it over with."

"The man's right." It was Wagner again. "He's a stinkin' Indian, a horse thief, and a killer." Wagner mounted his horse, and several men made a move toward theirs.

Braddock raised his voice. "You men just stay where you are. I'm not forming a posse." At that moment, he was pleasantly surprised to see Garvey positioned at the corner of Gunnison's Mercantile, a shotgun at the ready.

Wagner spoke up again. He had just enough saloon support to loosen him up. "Who's gonna hold these men here after you ride off, Marshal? You know I'll try my damnedest, but I doubt they'll listen." Wagner had his attention diverted by Reuben and was unaware of Garvey's shotgun, but the men poised to ride posse had not missed that detail. There was a decided lessening of interest in mounting horses.

Braddock was tired and a long day stretched ahead of him. He had had all of Vance Wagner he could take. "You'll do what? They've already got a craw full of you."

Wagner had a smirk on his face that he couldn't wipe off. "I'll bet we find Pickett before you do."

That was as far as he got. "And I'll bet that you don't ride with a posse this fine day," said Braddock

Grabbing Wagner by the shirt, he pulled him off the horse, dumped him in the dusty street on his shoulder. Wagner crawled under the hitching rack.

Horses and men pulled away from them. Wasting no time and leaving no opening, Reuben bulled through the hitch rack, tearing it from the ground, and catching it in both hands, he drove it straight into Wagner's gut. Wagner buckled at the knees, regained his balance, and crawled onto the boardwalk.

Throwing the rack aside, Braddock attempted to climb onto the walkway. Wagner threw a kick that landed heavily on Reuben's thigh slowing his rush momentarily. He recovered and caught Wagner's boot twisting him off balance. Still holding onto the boot, Braddock scrambled onto the boardwalk and drove Wagner headfirst into the saloon wall. Wagner recovered enough to throw an overhand right that Reuben took on a shoulder. Reuben pinned Wagner against the wall and pounded away at the ribs with both fists. It took all the starch out of Wagner. His eyes glazed over, and he sagged to the walkway.

Reuben was arm weary. His legs were trembling. Sweat soaked his shirt and ran into his eyes. It was time to quit, but he was not about to let Wagner off that easily. Grabbing a couple of ragged breaths and wiping the sweat from his eyes with his shirt sleeve, he pulled Wagner to his feet. Wagner tried to free his right hand and go for his pistol, but Braddock jerked it from the holster and sent it skittering down the boardwalk toward Garvey.

"No, you don't. And you don't get to quit like that. When I say no posse, I mean no posse." Starting with *when*, each word was accompanied by a blow to Wagner's middle. Nine blows in all. The Rocking R foreman slumped to the walk again. This time he was unconscious. Outside of the kick, he hadn't managed a solid blow. Just the way Reuben wanted it.

Reuben frisked him and found a holdout derringer in the left boot. He stood over Wagner and spoke to him as though he could hear every word. "You won't be needing this, and you won't be leading a posse. Those ribs'll keep you off a horse for a while."

Transferring the derringer to his left hand to keep the right hand free, he faced the crowd. "You men are too quick to reach for a rope. You might do better to step lightly, to remember back. Some of you've come close to stretching a rope yourselves." He paused looking at each man in turn. "I know who you are, each and every one of you. If you try to form a posse without my say so, I'll jail you. Or Garvey will."

The men melted away, leaving Reuben standing over Wagner. He thanked Garvey for the cover. "You likely kept them from doing something foolish. I'd be pleased if you'd serve as deputy while I'm gone. You can start by hauling this man off to the pokey on charges of inciting to riot. We'll look into murder charges when I get back. Post a guard around the clock. You'll have to hire a pair of deputies. See Trundle and Gunnison for the money. When I get back, we'll move Wagner to Silvercrown."

14

Trailing the roan he'd ridden that morning and riding a tough little dapple gray, Braddock traveled north on Little Willow River to the scene of the carriage wreck. Doc Miller was there helping recover the crumpled body of the banker's boy.

The matched pair of blacks had been dragged from the water. They were already beginning to bloat. Flies had found them and were pestering all present whether dead or alive. Bits of the carriage could be seen in the gravelly bottom of the stream. There were tracks of horses and men everywhere both above and below the bridge. Trying to find answers in that mess appeared hopeless and, at any event, would have to wait.

Braddock dismounted and joined Doc Miller at the crumpled form of the banker's son. Miller looked up from the corpse and said, "This ain't right, Reuben. A youngster killed like this. He was hardly half grown. A terrible waste. We can ill afford the loss of young ones like Jimmy. Our future rests squarely in their hands. And the Pickett boy . . . we'll likely lose him too. Why the hell he'd do a thing like this tops me."

"Billy Pickett had no hand in this at all."

"Who then?"

"Wagner. Hangs out at the Mountain View."

"Tall, slick looking, wears his gun low?"

Reuben nodded.

"I'm not surprised. You look at that cluster of maggots that hangs out at the Mountain View, you wonder if they were born of woman." Miller looked up at Reuben, waiting for a comment.

"Maggots is right. I've charged Wagner. Jailed him. But I need to find Billy and get his testimony before we lose him too."

"There's a wagon coming for Jimmy. We'll see to things here. You go find that boy."

"Who's going to talk to the banker?"

"He's already been here. He's home trying to comfort the wife. This'll play hell with her. Jimmy was their only child."

Reuben stopped in the middle of the bridge and looked downstream checking Billy's story. Sure enough, from the river behind Maria's where Billy and Tad White had been fishing, you could see the entire bridge. He looked on the north side of the bridge for the bushes that would support the Blankenship boy's story. There were none close enough to be a factor. For whatever reason, the boy was lying.

Braddock crossed the bridge and headed north to the Pickett place. It sat on a sunny south slope a few hundred yards above the river. The rutted road to the house had seen heavy, recent travel. He rode past a copse of pines and a small fenced grain field and into the yard. What he saw was sickening. The yard had been churned up by several horses. The house had been shot up. The family dog lay shot through the hips and had died trying to crawl to the meager shade of the kitchen porch. Further inspection showed the milk goat shot dead in its pen and chickens dead in various parts of the yard.

The destruction resembled a rampage by wayward boys or ravaging by dog packs. But to his mind, this was worse. Everywhere there was evidence of a malicious, destructive hatred that reeked of revenge. Vance Wagner had a lot to answer for. In the short time they had been at the Pickett place, Wagner's vigilantes had gone a long way toward destroying the Pickett's ability to support themselves. It reminded him of Kit Carson's treatment of the Navajo.

Braddock banked his anger. With Wagner jailed, the vigilantes or "posse," or whatever they considered themselves to be, would be without a leader. What discouraged him was the fact that a new leader was apt to emerge at any point. It was like killing a snake that could grow new heads at will.

15

With the boy on his mind, he took one last look at the desolated Pickett homestead and followed a deer trail over the mountain to its intersection with the Military Road.

Once under way, as he often did on lonely trails, he talked to the horses. "Well, boys," he said (actually, they were both mares), "we've got a bedroll, slicker, food, and water for the three of us for a week. What we don't have is a chance of catching up to that boy for at least two days, that's for sure."

It helped immensely knowing that the boy was headed for Yancey's Lazy Y. It meant that at some point Billy would turn north across the Alvordo Desert. To do that, only three trails made sense. He would search closely where those trails left the Military Road.

He was not surprised when he hit the road to the Ketchum Mine, where, except for heavy ore wagons, there had been no recent travel. Billy would have shunned it anyway to avoid the chance some mine personnel would spot him. He noted that Billy was already thinking like a hunted man.

One small unshod horse had continued on past the mine road. Braddock dismounted. Holding the reins and squatting in the scrap of shade the mare threw, he examined the tracks. There in the right front hoof was a small chip and a crack, the same print he'd seen in Maria's backyard. It was the boy's horse, and that presented a new problem. He sucked in his breath and scanned the vastness of the desert that lay before him. If that cracked hoof opened, the horse would grow lame, and Billy would be marooned out there, afoot in the great Alvordo wasteland, and worse yet, he'd have a horse to find water for, a horse he couldn't ride.

Braddock's little caravan made good progress for the next hour or so. Then, with the afternoon wearing seriously away, he came to the second northbound trail. It struck straight up through the basin. Of the three, it was the fastest route but also the riskiest. Nothing grew on those alkaline flats, and though the smooth basin floor stretched before the rider with the promise of fast travel, it was dangerous travel since there simply was no water. No good water. But if you were prepared and the day was not too hot, a five-hour charge into that basin got you across. It was much faster than the third route, which wound its tortuous way through Old Woman Mountain. So if you had a need for speed, if you were set on traveling the central route and you had a full moon like this night had in store, you could travel this piece in the cool of the night.

The gray's prints turned north. Billy had chosen. Braddock followed for the better part of an hour. It was turning cool, and for a little while, their travel speed picked up. Then, with the light beginning to fail, he came to a spot where it appeared the little gray refused to go on. There was a confusing bit of backtracking and a skirting of lava cliffs. Here the sign led him on a twisted, convoluted route that followed no trail, wasted time, and seemed to serve no purpose at all. Braddock was puzzled. Why would Billy abandon the trail?

He rode to the top of a narrow ridge to get a view of the basin ahead. Once he gained the ridgetop, he understood the wandering route. The basin ahead of the central trail was flooded with murky water. Somewhere in the far-off mountains, thunderstorms had triggered flash floods, turning the basin into a treacherous waste of quicksands and sulfurous mires.

He dismounted and pulled the saddle off the mare. Next, he gave each horse a nosebag full of water and hobbled them. Time to settle for the night.

Braddock looked again at the flooded basin to the north. He had seen flooding like this before. From his cowboy days, there tugged at his memory the plight of two pairs of Bar X stock caught in such a mire.

He had picked up the trail of several head on a slope dotted with piñon and followed it down a narrow trail that intersected with the main route to the Keller Rim. There in a little swale, bedded out of the wind, he found six pairs of Bar X stock. With a comforting bit of cussing and a lot of help from the bay, he started them down the trail to the

Rim. Not satisfied that he had them all, he returned to the intersection of the trails and spent some time checking their back trail. "Pay mind to what's about you. Even the desert will give up secrets if you give it a chance." His father's voice so insistent those days, prodding, suggesting, conspiring.

He saw at a considerable distance a pall of circling buzzards. Despite a dust storm that was beginning to build and was sending most creatures to cover, the buzzards were circling low over the basin ahead.

He picked his way across a flinty wash and up a small rise. Just ahead, evil-smelling pools of shallow water had trapped two pairs of Bar X stock. They were belly down in the muck. Even if the water receded in the next few hours, the cattle were doomed. They'd lose circulation in their feet and legs and be unable to walk. Most likely, it was already too late.

Soon black hordes of buzzards were dropping out of the sky and settling in the rocks. He'd been told that they were a blessing, that they kept the desert clean. He accepted that as true, knew their value, but he could not bring himself to like them. They were packing in around him now like undertakers at a convention, and he could smell them, smell the death they waded in.

He couldn't rid the desert of them, he decided, but he might cheat them of their noisome feast. He set his jaw and went about the task of rescuing the stock.

The nearest calf was easy. Although it was mired to its belly in a soupy mix, he was able to settle a rope over its neck from a cautious thirty feet away. Taking a wrap around the saddle horn, he clucked at the big bay. It backed slowly away pulling the calf from the mess. The mother bawled and lurched forward. He cursed. Her effort had only served to settle her more deeply into the muck.

He let the calf rest on its side, and to keep it from returning to the mire, he tied its feet with his neck bandana. Then he turned his attention to the cow. She was another ten feet out.

His first cast glanced off her shoulder and fell into the mud, but his second toss settled gratifyingly over her big horns. At first he tried to back up the bay as he'd done with the calf. It didn't budge her. The calf weighed in at three hundred pounds or so, but the cow, she had to top six hundred pounds. Maybe seven. He longed to get behind her and give her tail a twist. That'd move her. On his next pull, she clawed at the muck, found something solid, came to her feet, then fell to the side. The big bay wasted no time sliding her out of the muck. Once out, she made it to her knees. Dismounting, he shook loose his lariat. The big cow made a feeble effort to hook him with her wicked set of horns, but she was no threat. He freed the calf and remounted.

It was hotter now and the flies were gathering as thick as the buzzards. He mopped at his brow and waited. For a scary few minutes, it seemed that she lacked the will to rise. If she didn't get up, he'd have wasted his time. She'd die where she rested. Without her, the calf would have little chance to survive. Soon though, with her calf bawling again, she lunged twice and rocked to her feet. Wavering *but determined, without a backward look, she put the calf ahead of her down the trail to the Keller Rim.*

When it came to the second pair, the undertakers won.

Braddock shook his head. The past had closed in on him for a few moments. Never mind that little lapse; the past was always with us, wasn't it? He searched about on the rocky shelf for a place to make his bed.

16

Elder Creek's jail had started life as a root cellar. It had walls of quarried stone that lined a hole dug into the riverbank. Sawdust put into the ceiling by way of insulation leaked through the planks and onto the floor and onto the prisoner. Sometime in the past, it had acquired an oak door with barred windows. High in the eastern wall was a small barred window that provided cross ventilation. Despite the additions, it was a shackled-together affair that hardly deserved to be called a jail.

After Wagner's pounding by Braddock, he had been thrown with little ceremony onto a wagon bed and carted there. He had groaned and whimpered most of the three blocks' ride.

His only visitors that first day were Deputy Garvey and Doc Miller. The latter brought him a half-pint of whiskey and told him to stay off a horse for a week to give the ribs a chance to heal. "Get lots of rest, and for tonight, use this whisky to fight back the pain. Best thing I've got for it. Rotgut, I suppose, but it's what the Mountain View had. As to the future, if I was you, I'd pure and simple stay away from Marshal Braddock."

The first day of his incarceration, Wagner was too miserable to care where he was. Midway through the second morning, after Garvey had brought food and fresh water, Wagner got another visitor.

"Vance, Vance, you there?" Pelham peered down into the hole. "It's me, Ace."

Wagner rolled over on the narrow cot. "Yeh, I'm here. Been tryin' to figure just where, though."

"Where? Jail."

Wagner seemed to consider that for a moment. "Doesn't look like a jail. More like a cellar."

"It's what they've got. Like I told ya, me and the boys burned out the last sheriff, jail and all. 'Fore you got here. You're here because you decided to take on Braddock."

More groans. "So I did. I'd a whipped him too, but he sneaker punched me."

Pelham struggled a little trying to work that statement in with his memory of the brawl. Wagner lurched to a sitting position. His boot caught the empty pint bottle and sent it clattering across the damp stone floor.

Peering back into the depths of the cellar, Pelham spoke up again. "Braddock said he did it to keep you from gathering a posse."

"Yeh? Well, it won't work. Won't." He paused for a breath. Deep breaths were not possible. "Tomorrow sure, I'll ride."

Pelham stood up straight to ease his back. He looked out across the river at a sagebrush flat and a broad swatch of blue sky. He looked back in at Wagner and shook his head. He was thinking that there had to be a better way to get what you wanted than to lock horns with the law, especially when Braddock was the law. He swore there and then that he'd add a little more to his nest egg and clear out of Elder Creek for good. Let Braddock have it.

Wagner thought Pelham was leaving. "What are ya up to now? Just get me outta here."

"That's what I come to tell ya. We can't spring ya until tonight."

"Why the hell not? You think this is some damn hotel?"

"We'll get you out all right, but you need to know, folks are spittin' mad about us shootin' up the Pickett place."

"Let'm get mad. We don't owe 'em nothing'"

"I'm just telling you, it warn't a good idea. You shoulda held the boys in. I also come to tell ya, Braddock has gone to get the Pickett boy. I trailed him till he cut off north on Old Woman Mountain."

"Took the trail through Old Woman Mountain?"

Pelham didn't bother to answer. Just stared back at him.

Wagner added, "I ain't callin' you a liar, it's just . . . I've heard that's the hard way."

"Hard and slow. I've been on it. Me and Pard Rogers took a few head of borrowed stock that way. Right now they's been a flash flood. Turned some of the desert floor into a mess of mud and stink water. Can't travel there, so Braddock took the Old Woman Trail. Point is, when he catches the kid, he'll have to come back the same trail, and he'll be ending up at Morning Glory Wells. But we don't have to go on the mountain. All we gotta do is wait for them at the Wells. You can't hardly let that boy back here. He's connected you to the carriage wreck."

Wagner had a headache, and his ribs hurt. Pelham was annoying him. "I see all that, Pelham. I see that. Braddock know you were following him?"

"Tracked him, more like. I was two, three hours behind. I just made sure where he was goin' and come back here to get you out. But, as I said, that's gotta wait till dark. You can use my room at the Mountain View. We'll break you outta here, bring you a horse."

"Horse? I'm not ridin' no horse. Not tonight. Sonofabitchin' marshal saw to that. Did I tell ya? I'm gonna kill him soon as I see him."

"Won't be soon. We might have to wait awhile for him at the Wells. But we'll get both him and the kid. Nobody'll ever know just what happened way out there. We'll spring you tonight, and things'll look better."

17

Lamps were being lit in the parlors of Elder Creek, and shadows were growing long when Garvey approached the jail. He was carrying Wagner's supper and a fresh half-pint of rotgut sent by the doc. He had been happier when his prisoner slept his hours away. But tonight Wagner was rattling a tin cup against the bars and raising such a fuss that Simpson, the guard with the afternoon shift, should have responded. But he hadn't. In fact, there was no Simpson in sight. Garvey presumed that the man had abandoned his post. Quietly cussing Simpson for not providing backup, he set down his lantern and reached for his key ring. The slightest noise behind him warned him but too late. As he turned, the night fell in on him. There was a great roaring in his head, an awful swirling pain at the base of his skull. He wanted to fight back but was in and out of consciousness for the next many minutes.

Soon he was aware that he was being dragged behind a horse, that the back of his coat had ridden up and he was losing skin to the dirt and gravel of the street. He twisted so that his left side took the bulk of the damage. He pulled his right arm free and reached to his holster but his revolver was gone. He passed out again.

At the livery stable, Garvey's hands were untied, and he was thrown half conscious into a stall with a large draft horse. His attackers goaded the terrified horse with a broom handle. The horse rolled its eyes and danced trying frantically to avoid his tormentors.

Halfway to the creek, Simpson lay bleeding to death in a ditch.

The snow-draped peaks of the Sierras had finally given up their light for the day, and most creatures had taken to their beds when a carriage pulled to a stop in the alley by the Mountain View saloon. A few horses still stood at the hitch racks, the pale orange glow of coal oil lamps leaked out under the batwing doors. But the street was empty when Vance Wagner freshly sprung from the storm cellar was helped down from the carriage and to the outside stairs by Ace Pelham. Wagner shrugged off further help. Grabbing the handrail of the outside stairs, he turned to Pelham. "Bring me a pint and some grub. Tell the boys we'll ride at daybreak. I'll need you to bring the black around ready to go. Extra horses. We'll go hunting."

Pelham was in good spirits. Once inside the saloon, he went straight to the bar and shoved his way between the two men that helped him break Wagner loose. He told them of Wagner's plans for the morning. Catching the bartender's attention, he ordered food and a pint of whiskey to take up to Wagner. "And," he said, "get me and the boys some good whiskey and keep the beer flowing. We're gonna do a little celebrating."

Ace Pelham was having trouble containing his enthusiasm because the way things were going, the way he saw it, he would soon be leading the gang again and in control of the money that came with it. The way he figured, Wagner would shoot it out with the marshal. If Wagner died in the gunfight, one Ace Pelham would emerge as the leader. If Wagner killed the marshal, a swarm of law would be after him, and he'd either leave the country or swing from a cottonwood. Same result. Pelham figured he couldn't lose. He'd be in the chips. One good payoff and he'd catch a stage to Reno and the big time.

Just down the bar, Tap Trundle was listening to a cattle buyer with one ear and to Pelham with the other. He caught Sonny's attention, leaned over the bar, and said softly, "They've sprung Wagner and will ride at daybreak. That means I've got some organizing to do. Keep the gang drinking if you can. And, Sonny, set a fresh beer in front of me like I was coming back." He slipped out the back door. Ahead of him was a long, hard ride in the dark of the night.

18

Just as though he'd heard Tap Trundle's call, Pat Beacher made a rare night trip to town. That afternoon, he'd oiled his Winchester, tied a bedroll on behind the saddle cantle, and stuffed his saddlebags with jerky and dried apples. Satisfied that he was travel ready, he looked for Krebs and found him packing water to the chickens. "I'm leaving you in charge, Whitey. I know you can do it. I've got me an itch to see if Wagner is still safely in the pokey. If he isn't, neither of us is safe. You stick close to the house and corrals. Mend some tack, fix a gate. Do the chores. Just don't leave the place until I'm back. Unless Wagner shows up. If he does, you hide out till he's gone. No hero crap, you hear me? Figure on me bein' gone a coupla, three, four days."

The roan gelding fell into an easy, energy-conserving trot. Krebs watched as horse and rider disappeared into the gathering darkness. The unsettling bark of a fox high on the ridge behind the henhouse set the mood. Krebs was alone on the big ranch.

19

Back in Elder Creek, Maria came out of a deep sleep, a scream dying in her throat. She looked wildly about. It was her bedroom, but she had half expected to be somewhere else. She lit her bedside lamp; warm light filled the corners of her room. All was right with the room. What wasn't right was the dream. It was the usual dream of Reuben and the shadowy figure, but it had changed. This time shots were fired. This time there was a body in the dust.

She dressed hurriedly and went straight to kitchen and poked up the fire in the woodstove.

"That you, Maria?" It was Bonnie calling from the storage room where she slept on a canvas cot.

"Just hold tight, Bonnie. I couldn't sleep. Puttin' on coffee."

"I'll be right there." Bonnie emerged in another minute in a light robe Maria had given her.

"You've got some nerve," said Maria, trying to lighten the mood. "That robe never looked like that when I wore it."

"Like I said, you've got your brand on the marshal, I get nothing but bad offers." Bonnie rubbed her eyes. "I can't get to sleep either, Maria. I got to wondering about Billy, and of course, you were in there screaming in your sleep."

Maria ground coffee beans. "It's the same dream. The bad one. Reuben and that damn gunslinger. I'm making a big pot, strong and black. Then I'm gonna make a batch of biscuits. While I'm cooking, we'll do some thinking. We've got to figure some way we can take a hand in this mess."

Pat Beacher pounded his way toward town. He was nursing a grudge, and it had to do with Vance Wagner. As he looked back on it, he had been due to inherit the foreman job at the Rocking R. He'd worked hard and was, by all accounts, deserving. Then Wagner had come along. Twice they'd fought. Beacher, essentially a man of peace, did not carry a sidearm, so they'd fought bare-knuckle; each time, Beacher lost to the bigger man. Instead of firing Wagner and ridding the place of the troublemaker, Reno Rawlins, owner of the rocking R, had named him foreman. So much for loyalty.

Beacher tried to be bitter at Rawlins, but he understood; Rawlins was no gunfighter either. But the fact remained that Wagner was. He carried a pearl-handled revolver and a reputation to go with it.

Besides his need to settle the grudge, Beacher wanted to offer Braddock a hand. It was a loyalty he found hard to explain, but it was there. Maybe it was because Braddock made him feel that better times could be had, that things could be set right. Whatever was coming, and you could feel things building, Beacher wanted to side with the law. And if Wagner was out of the picture at the end, so much the better.

He arrived at the Mountain View saloon just as Tap was coming down the alley between the saloon and Gunnison's. Tap gestured up the street, and they rode off toward Tap's shop before speaking. "You saved me a trip, Pat. I've got to organize a little help. They've broken Wagner out of the pokey, and the Mountain View bunch plans to ride in the morning. Gonna ambush Reuben and the kid if they find them."

"You can count on me. It's what I rode in for. I had to know what Wagner was up to."

"Well then, Pat, suppose you go try to get Gunnison to help. Then wait with him at my place. I'll go find Garvey. Could be he's home taking it easy."

When Beacher and Gunnison entered Tap's blacksmith shop, they were surprised to see Bonnie Pickett waiting. They shared versions of the day's events while a worrisome half hour dragged by. Where was Tap?

Tap and Garvey showed together, Garvey favoring his right leg. His face was cut and bruised. Three men had jumped him, he said. It happened on the path leading to the jail where he'd gone to relieve the watch.

"They drug me behind a horse clear to the livery, then threw me into a stall with a jittery horse. They poked at that horse with a broom handle until he went near crazy, jumping and stomping and me under him the whole time. They left me for dead."

While he was relating his woes, Tap was cleaning the cuts on Garvey's back. "Oh, lordy, Tap. Go a little easy there."

"Sure. Just you hold still."

"Sorry. Crazy thing is, all the time that horse was stomping, it knew where I was. Never stepped on me once. No thanks to them. They meant to kill me, make it look like an accident. I'm sure of it. It's just one more reason to put an end to that vigilante group."

Tap looked around at the gathering. "So we know for sure that Wagner is loose. Should we go after him?"

Garvey shook his head. "He's loose all right, but they've got several guns besides his to keep it that way. Taking them head-on wouldn't be smart."

"Those men that got Wagner out, could you tell who they were?" asked Beacher.

"It was Ace Pelham," said Garvey. "Pelham and the rest of the Mountain View hangouts. Sonny knows them. I guess you know, they plan to ride in the morning."

Bonnie interrupted, "We got wind of that down at Maria's. Suppose we put a stop to their ride?"

Tap replied without giving it much thought, "Like Garvey said, they are quite a force when they get together. Too many guns."

"I suppose so," Bonnie replied, her voice filled with a quiet resolve, "but I'm guessing there's a way to thin them out before they gather to ride."

Tap Trundle looked over at Bonnie. It was as if he'd seen her for the first time. She was bent slightly forward toward the light from the forge. Her long dark hair framed her serious face; her brown eyes held a challenge. So many times he'd seen her on the street and dismissed her as the Indian woman selling baskets. In this light and this close up, he saw her beauty, felt her strength. "Thin them out? Suppose you tell us your plan, Bonnie, while I brew some coffee beans."

Later he was to say, "I felt the power of her presence, and it had an extraordinary effect on me. I stopped thinking it was a matter for men to decide and accepted her as an equal. Good thing I did."

20

Reuben's left knee where Wagner had kicked him was swollen and threatened to buckle under him; still he took time to water and feed the horses from the supply of rolled oats he'd brought. Only then did he turn to his own needs. He picked out a runty sagebrush and watered its roots. He was surprised at how little pee there was. He'd have to remember to drink more often and to mind that the horses had more water too.

Supper was an apple and a slice of beef rolled in a tortilla. He ate the beef, pulling from time to time on a water jug. Above him, the faithful stars danced in the desert sky. He settled his great coat about him and searched for the little dipper, his favorite constellation. He was sitting on his slicker with the one wool blanket he'd allowed himself draped across his legs. He had discarded the idea of using the saddle blanket as a ground cover. It was still wet from the sweat of the horse.

He'd been in the saddle since morning, a morning that seemed far away now, and he was so tired he decided against eating the apple and stuffed it into the pocket of his coat. His knee was less painful now, but it was stiffening. Morning would be hell. He found a patch of sand to bed in and positioned himself with his head uphill on a slight slope. Using the saddle as a pillow, he lay back and pulled his hat down over his eyes. In minutes, he was asleep and then, grudgingly, back half awake. Somehow a rock had worked its way up through the sand and was poking his hip. He struggled to a slightly higher position, squirming away from one rock only to find another. He'd have cursed if it was likely to do any good.

In minutes, he was asleep again but not before he remembered back to the night just last week that he'd spent in Maria's bed with cool, clean-smelling sheets, the warm, musky scent of Maria. She had rubbed his back and shoulders, crawled in, and drawn him to her. Why would a man trade that for pile of rocks?

Charlie Prescott had nailed it. "Find yourself a good woman and stick with her," he had said. There was truth in a good woman's arms, a fundamental honesty. He had found it once before, only to lose it. Now he had found it again. And again, as so many times before, the badge called, and he was sleeping in a rock pile. But he wouldn't mess it up this time. He'd go back to Maria as soon as this was over. He'd find a preacher and tie the knot good and proper. Soon as he found Billy. Soon as they hung Wagner . . . Soon as . . .

He awoke chilled. The sky was a pearly gray slowly giving away to lemon. He got carefully to his feet and walked about the confines of the ledge, working the stiffness out of the knee. He suffered from a puzzle of pains, each endeavoring to outdo the other and no way to guess which would win out.

He pushed the pain aside, spoke to the horses. "You boys ready to head out?" Silly question. It was their impatient stamping most likely that had awakened him. More oats, more water. He rubbed each horse down with the saddle blanket, then saddled the gray before eating sparingly of his tortilla and meat supplies. It felt good to move about.

He fiddled around getting everything in good order before risking the trail ahead. It would be full of drop-offs, shale slides, and dry gorges. Any sort of hurry or inattention could mean a nasty fall. *Play the cards dealt to you, but keep the odds on your side.* When full light came on, when he could tell a white hair from a black hair, they set out north on Old Woman Mountain.

21

Ahead a mile or so, Reuben saw circling buzzards. It signaled trouble for something or someone. All the way there, he tried to sort out the possibilities. Billy might have killed a deer and left the guts for the buzzards, but food and water were in such short supply that there were few deer on the mountain. Besides, Billy would know not to risk firing a gun and drawing attention to himself, and it was not likely to be a cow down this far from any spread with Yancey's Flying Y still a long day's ride away. Try as he might to find other answers, it was probably the horse and rider ahead of him that had caused the gathering of carrion fowl.

He hurried the best he could all the while being nagged by the thought that he was somehow responsible for the fact that Billy was riding for his life.

The going here was very rough. A rim of palisades shut off upslope traffic. The intrusion of talus masses at the base of the palisades every few hundred feet forced the trail to dip into sharply eroded gullies.

Reuben pressed on. As he grew closer to the circling birds, he could see that they were still few in number. Maybe if it was Billy that had drawn the attention of the buzzards, he had holed up for some reason. Maybe horse and rider were having problems but were alive. He clung to that idea.

Braddock descended into a steep, dry gully that challenged both horse and rider. It was near the bottom of that pitch that he discovered Billy's boot prints. Reuben looked more closely. Sign on the trail showed that the gray had gone lame and that Billy was leading it. Braddock hurried up the trail, picked his way along the bottom of another talus. When he reached the ridgetop, he was able to look into the next ravine. His hopes sank. Deep in the gully, he could make out the crumpled heap of the gray horse. The gully's dry bed was filled with rocks the size of sheep. From where he was, he could not see Billy. He dismounted and led his horses trying as he descended the trail to read the story.

At this point on the trail, Billy was still walking ahead of the gray, and the gray was still having trouble with his footing. Braddock came to the spot where the gray had tumbled and rolled off a ledge, bounced off a rock, and plummeted into the gully below. It was a bad fall. Life taking. The sure-footed gray had fallen to his death, and if the boy was walking here, he'd left no sign of it. If Billy had decided to ride down this pitch, he'd be lying under that horse.

The way to the horse's crumpled body involved a pair of switchbacks that he endured only too aware that to hurry here was to flirt with disaster. When he finally reached the bottom, there was no sign of Billy. Other than a shattered saddle, the only thing he could find under the horse was a smashed canteen. There was no saddle blanket or bridle. The gray had a broken leg and massive damage to the ribs on one side. The sand around its head was dark with dried blood. He looked more closely. Billy had cut its throat to end its misery. It was a good sign. Billy had survived.

He tried to flex the horse's leg. It was stiff and the carcass was cold. The horse had died late afternoon or evening the day before. For nearly a day, Billy had been afoot on Old Woman Mountain and most likely out of water.

Reuben walked the horses around the corpse and remounted. They labored up the path and out of the gully. He would be cautious now, for somewhere ahead he would find Billy, but it would be a Billy armed with the old double-barrel and very touchy about his back trail.

22

Billy had not been on the gray when it fell, but he had an ankle sprain from careening down the slope after the gray only to find when he got there that it was terribly injured and thrashing about in its pain. Avoiding the thrashing feet, he had jumped on the horse's neck, grabbed a solid handful of mane, and cut a deep slash in the throat. Obeying an impulse, he caught blood in his cupped hand and drank it. Drank the blood of the strong. Cleaning his hands in the sand, he managed a last look at the gray and struck out on foot headed north.

By nightfall, Billy's small canteen was empty. He spent a miserable night huddled in the horse's blanket a few feet above the bottom of a gully. At long last, false dawn broke in the east. While he waited for better light, he ate a cold tortilla and a little jerky. He was still hungry but decided to wait for water before he ate more jerky.

He struggled in and out of two dry ravines. The ankle growing more painful, swelling again. Topping the second ravine, the first sunlight of the day fell on a copse of birch trees with swatches of green grass all about. He hobbled his way there and drank his fill from a small stream and filled his remaining canteen before settling into the shade of willows. His next thoughts were of the gray—if only he could have gotten him to this spot, turned him loose here.

He ate more jerky and tortillas, chewed carefully and thoughtfully, enjoying the food he'd carried. For the moment, he was comfortable, his thirst quenched by the good, clear water. But it was not a time to celebrate. He was on foot, his ankle was throbbing from the morning walk, and with the small canteen that remained to him, he would be unable to travel in the desert. Until his ankle healed, he had to stay with this water supply and eat what food he could find. And what about his back trail? Was Wagner riding it?

There were things he could be reasonably sure of: anyone arriving on his back trail would be on a horse, they would not arrive after dark, and they were not likely to arrive in the early morning, but the rest of the day was dangerous. He had to wait in ambush where the short range of the shotgun would be effective. As an additional circumstance, he had but five loads for the gun. Using the gun to gather food was out. It might be heard anyway. He'd have to set snares for rabbits, and there would be frogs. The place was loud with them. Maybe the pond had trout. At any rate, his present supply of tortillas would last until the next morning.

He spent a half hour destroying any sign that he had entered the meadow from the south. The trail swung just above the ponds and crossed through the aspens. Because of swampy ground, a rider was not apt to travel below the ponds. He chose a slot between two rocks and just below the trail. Anyone approaching from the south would crest the ridge about forty paces from his fortification. When the rider reached the edge of green grass, he would be just thirty paces away and in perfect range. The trick was to get rid of the man without harming the horse.

Midmorning now and he would have to stay in position. If more than one rider came, his situation would be desperate. There would be but one. Two at the most. He willed himself to believe that.

The sun was bringing a pleasant warmth to the little meadow. The blackbirds and frogs along the pond's edge and in the cattails were making their music. He dozed with the big gun nested in the rocks in front of him.

Sometime later, he jerked awake with a suddenness that frightened him. But there was nothing on the trail. What had alerted him? Was it a hoof hitting stone? He waited. It was deathly quiet. Only the wind sighing in the cattails. That was it: the frogs and the blackbirds had gone silent. It was the quiet that woke him. He snicked back both hammers of the ten gauge and trained them on the path. Another sound. A small sound. He wondered at being aware of such small warnings. From his mother's people?

He was thirsty, and his right leg had gone to sleep, but he didn't dare take his eyes off the trail.

Soon a black hat appeared. Then the top half of the man under it. Then horse and man fully before him in the sun. There was a second horse being trailed. They were reaching the edge of the grass. He would have to fire soon, moved his finger to the trigger. He had the neck and shoulders of the man covered.

The man stopped, called out, "Yo, Billy. You there?"

Billy stared. Then he saw the sun glinting off a marshal's badge. He eased the hammers down, let the gun rest in the rocks, and stood up. He forgot his bad ankle and started to run. The horse sidled away. Billy hobbled to a stop in the middle of the trail. "Marshal, it's me, Billy."

The hair rose on the back of Braddock's neck. He had hoped to find the boy here, but the ambush had been so perfect. If it hadn't been the boy . . . If it had been Wagner . . . "Good God, Billy. You gave me a fright."

They watered the horses and let them graze an hour on the sweet grass surrounding the pond. While the animals grazed, they shared accounts of their trips through the desert. Billy explained why he took to Old Woman Mountain. "It was the little gray that saved me. I wanted to travel the quick trail up the middle. But he wouldn't go there."

"I'm sorry that you lost the gray. He surely was a good horse, Billy, and likely saved your life. It's like the roan here. I owe her plenty."

Billy had been watching for the beginning of shadows in the palisades. He pointed to them and said, "We are losing the morning, Marshal."

"Your point is well taken, Billy. If we strike off down the trail now, we should make Morning Glory Wells in time to set up camp. I sure don't want another dry camp in a rock pile. Let's refill these canteens and hit the trail."

23

The following morning, early light was breaking over the low hills to the east when Wagner and Ace Pelham swaggered out of the Mountain View. A small muted group of riders awaited them. Faces covered with kerchiefs, slicker collars pulled up, and hats snugged down tight, they sat their horses in a tight circle and shivered in the chilly desert air. Wagner took a pull at a pint of whiskey, capped it, and shoved it in a saddlebag. Fortified, he drew himself up into the saddle with great difficulty, nodded at the assembled riders, and with Pelham at his side, set out for Morning Glory Wells.

In that same morning chill, from his ridgetop vantage point, Braddock peered down into the funnel-shaped holes that were known as Morning Glory Wells. The water appeared gray this early, but before long, it would resemble the bright blue of its namesake. He and the boy were marooned on the ridge north of the Military Road and above the springs because camped on the green swath below the wells was a small band of Indians. Small, but three of them were armed with rifles, maybe four if you figured one was acting as sentinel somewhere in the rocks. Reuben wanted to ride in on them and demand a share of the wells, but there might be a ruckus, and his forces, if you were honest about it, amounted to a gimpy-legged marshal and a tired boy. Besides, he had no quarrel with the Indians. He settled back looking at the world from under his battered gray hat. Maybe he could wait them out.

The boy, roused himself now, came to a sitting position and was peering down at the group at the springs. Where skin showed, he was a dark brown, almost black. *That's a lot of sun,* Braddock thought, *and a lot of Indian from his mother's side.* The boy was slight and not above five feet two or three, but at thirteen, he had time to grow. He wore ragged jeans with a long-sleeved blue shirt and hand-me-down work shoes. Someone, probably his mom, had neatly mended the shoes in several places with thin strips of rawhide. He wore a too-large buckskin jacket and a beaded headband tied about his coarse black hair.

A red ball of fire broke over the mountains to the east. It brought a warmth that was momentarily pleasing, but Reuben knew it to be deceptive. There was little shade on their perch, and soon enough the red ball would hang above them, turning their ridgetop into a bake oven. *Maybe,* Braddock thought, *the Indians will soon leave, and we'll bathe our feet in cool waters, fill our canteens.*

The morning wore on. Three or four buzzards settled onto the nearby rocks. For the second night running, Reuben had slept poorly. It had been cold causing him to bundle up in his big coat with the slicker under him. He'd given his blanket to Billy, so there was no cover for his legs. In his half sleep, he dreamed he was at Maria's café. She had served him a dish of beef and red peppers, which he was loading into tortillas hot off her stove. He was chasing them down with beer, but the whole thing was wrong. The beer tasted like rabbit brush, and although he pulled mightily at the earthenware mug, his thirst went unabated. The sun was warming the rocks. With the boy on watch, he snuggled deeper into the coat and dozed again.

Sometime later, he awoke to cracked lips and a tugging at his boot. The boy was after his attention. He was pointing east on the Military Road and toward Elder Creek. At first Braddock saw nothing, then he picked up what the boy's sharp eyes had found much earlier. A column of riders several miles out was headed for the Wells. His first thought was cavalry. No, hang that, they'd left six months back. "Billy," he spoke softly, his voice just above a whisper. "That can't be cavalry. Who the hell would it be?"

Needing no time to consider the question, Billy replied, "Wagner."

Reuben shook his head. "No, I don't think so. I put Wagner in jail. Besides, it looks like there are several riders in the group. Who'd come all the way out here with him?"

"Most likely he broke out of jail, and he's riding with that gang from the Mountain View. They'd follow him anywhere."

Braddock could think of no other possibility. He worried that over before answering, "If it's Wagner, we got a problem. How many riders do you figure?"

"It's too far, Marshal. I can't tell."

"Here, use my glass." So saying, he fished it out of the pocket of his great coat and handed it to Billy.

Billy waited for the riders to reappear from behind an outcrop of rock. "I count six riders trailing two or three extra mounts. They are coming at a good clip."

Braddock was sick at the thought. If it's the vigilantes, Billy was still in danger. So were the Indians. Braddock set to cussing. The way things turned out, he should have hauled Wagner to a proper cell in Silvercrown and found the boy later. For if the boy was right, if Wagner had escaped from jail, it meant that he'd found a way to get by Garvey. Could be that he'd put both Garvey and Billy in harm's way, made a mess of it all around.

From where he sat, there wasn't a good way out. In a little while, they'd have a bunch of hard-shooting men down their necks. He'd be swarmed over, and he couldn't do a damn thing about it. And the stubborn, ornery fact remained: if they got Billy, they'd hang him from the first tree they came to.

Yesterday, clearing the boy's name and putting Wagner away had seemed an easy enough thing to do. Justice would be served and the law satisfied. Now all that seemed in doubt, and once again Braddock felt the weight of the badge, felt alone.

He peered over the edge of the cliff at the group of Indians. They were not likely to help unless, of course, they'd take Billy south into the desert.

"Billy, it looks like those are your mother's people down there. Could you go to them? Join them?"

"I looked at them earlier. It's her band all right. What's left of it. But I couldn't go with them. I don't know them. Don't know the lingo. Besides, wouldn't that be just the same as running?" He turned and looked at Braddock. There was no answer. He shrugged and turned back to looking down on the Indian band. "Of course, I've thought about it before, thought of joining them . . . becoming part of that life. But it's not for me. There is no future in it, only past. I want a part in the future. And I want my name cleared."

"I'd like nothing more than that myself," replied Braddock. "But I guess I thought Garvey could keep Wagner in jail. Then I'd get you back safe and sound, and we'd get it all straightened out. But as it is, we've got six armed men coming after us. We can't win that one. And if they've come to hang you, and I can't stop them, why then, I've failed you. Can't have that either."

More carrion eaters settled in the rocks. Billy changed the subject. "Why are the buzzards coming here, Marshal?"

"Maybe they smell death, Billy."

"None of us dead."

"Not yet, but we can't sit up here all day. They know how to wait, the ugly buggers. They're good at it. And if things don't change, if the Indians don't leave, we'll run out of water, and even if we don't, those critters will give us away to Wagner's outfit. The only thing we can do now is send you back north with both horses. You might say we did all that damn work for nothing, but it's not true. We got some time in the desert together. I'm glad for that."

The boy gave Braddock a curious look. "I'll stay and fight with you. We can stop them."

"Not a chance, Billy. I made your mom a promise, and I'm gonna keep it. That means you gotta get the hell out of here. Now." He paused, waiting for Billy's answer. When it failed to come, he said, "You'll be helping me keep that promise. That means a good deal to me."

Billy hesitated, started to speak, then said nothing.

"Look at it this way, Billy. They've come out all this way to get you, but if you go north, they can't catch you. Not with those horses. Even the spares are tired. You've cheated them, cheated them out of their prey."

The marshal's reluctance to get into a showdown with Wagner's gang worried Billy. Maybe their chances weren't good. Insisting on sticking it out might mean they'd kill the marshal. Might mean that he, Billy, would be hung and the gang would get everything they wanted. It threw a light on his aunt's story about the willows on the river bank and made a good deal of sense: bend but don't break, be there when the storm passes.

"All right, Marshal. If I'm not here, you won't have to get in a shoot-out with them. I'll go, but I won't be on the run either. Not if I see it the way you see it. I'll wait it out at Yancey's."

Solemnly and with ceremony, the boy shook hands with Reuben, gathered the horses, and melted away north. He watched the boy out of sight, then looked down at the wells. The Indians had gone. He looked down the Military Road. The riders were just minutes away. Time to move. Time to meet the riders.

24

A nearly empty canteen slung across his left shoulder, Braddock struggled down the trail toward the Military Road. His knee was threatening to buckle, and he was having trouble with his eyes. He had allowed himself to dehydrate again. He muttered to himself, "Should've known better . . . all these years in the desert." He uncapped the canteen, tipped it up, and drained it. The water was warm as spit and left the taste of the metal in his mouth.

With the sound of approaching riders on his mind, he tried to hurry the last hundred feet of the trail, caught his boot heel on a sagebrush root, and fell full length into a gulley. The canteen clanged off one way, and he fell the other, landing heavily on his right side. The slide filled his holster with dirt and ground-in rocks. He scrambled to his feet. In a desperate hurry now, he had to be at the road before they got there, but first he had to deal with the gun. *Check the barrel, check the barrel.* The thought kept racing through his mind. He swung the cylinder open, checking the loads, brushing at the dirt. He broke a limb off a sagebrush and rammed it through the barrel. The clatter of the hooves was heavy on the road. The barrel was clean. He slapped the .44 shut. Made sure it revolved freely. With the tail of his shirt, he worked the dirt out of his holster. The hooves louder now.

He slid the gun in and out of the holster until it worked freely. He lurched to the middle of the road and glared toward the east. He heard the jingle of a bridle. The shuffle of hooves subsided as the lead rider pulled to a stop maybe thirty feet from him.

"Well, look who's here." It was Wagner. The voice was cracked, taunting. "Looks like you been rooting with the hogs, Marshal."

The dust from their progress blew over Braddock. He felt the grit settle on his face. It gave off a nasty chemical odor. He waited for the dust to settle. Once it did, he could see a little better, but he decided to string things out, get a better feel of the situation. The bulk of the riders had pulled up a good thirty paces behind the leader. There were likely a half dozen riders in all. "That you, Wagner?" The trick was to keep Wagner talking long enough to get his exact location, sort him out from the others. An ornery perversity had taken over Braddock. There was a job to do. A job he could still manage. Six gunmen to one? All right, so he'd go down in a hail of bullets, but he was damn sure going to take Wagner with him.

"So what if it is, Braddock? We come after the killer."

"Killer?"

"That horse thievin' Indian brat that killed the banker's boy."

"That's where you're wrong, Wagner." He raised his voice for the benefit of the other riders. "All the evidence points to you. Therefore, I'm ordering you, in the name of the State of Nevada, to throw down your arms! I'm arresting you for the murder of Jimmy Hodges."

"You're standing in the way of justice, Braddock. That's all you're doin'. Just step aside or I'll have to run you over."

"You resisting arrest? Seems like you've come a long way just to hear the gates of hell fly open."

"You'll be the one ridin' into hell, Marshal. If I don't get you, the boys will. That right, boys?"

There was no reply from the riders behind him. Silence stretched out. Wagner sat still as death watching Braddock's gun hand. If he had risked looking back, he'd have seen a rider come up close on either side of Pelham, seen his arms go up as a rifle barrel was jammed under his armpit on either side. Wagner didn't need to look to identify Tap Trundle's easy drawl. "Raise those hands, Pelham. You're settin' out this dance."

"What the hell?" It was Wagner. He was aware now that the balance had shifted.

A puzzled Braddock yelled out, "Get those hands up, Wagner."

With an enemy before him and now enemies behind him, Wagner felt the trap closing. Instead of giving up, he drove his horse at Braddock and clawed at his pistol. Reuben caught the movement and fired two rapid shots into the blur, twisting as he did so to avoid the horse. Too slow. He was bowled aside into the dust of the Military

Road. Wagner was blown out of the saddle, but his foot hung up in a stirrup, and his body was dragged until the terrified horse finally pulled to a stop.

Half a mile back and urging her team on, Maria drove a borrowed wagon. She had heard the shots and images from her most dreaded nightmares crowded before her. She applied her whip to the sweating horses. Her *Jefe* . . .

25

Nearly a week after the showdown at Morning Glory Wells, Reuben came blinking awake. Sun was streaming through the window of Maria's bedroom. He raised himself to one elbow for a moment. Deciding that his head was clear and his strength returned, he sat fully upright. There was stiffness and soreness in his left leg, but his vision was back, and he felt good, lazy almost. It sounded as if a crowd had gathered in the café. Soon the door eased open. It was Maria. She came to his bedside and ran a gentle hand over his forehead, popped another pillow behind his back. "So nice to see you, Maria." He kissed her hand.

She patted his hand. "So nice to see you sitting up. A few people here to visit with you, *Jefe*."

"A few? Sounds like a church social."

"You be nice. You need visitors."

Crowding into the small room behind Maria were Tap Trundle, Pat Beacher, Gunnison, Holmes, Garvey, and Bonnie with Billy at her side.

They nudged Billy to the front. He was first to speak. "Good to see you, Marshal Braddock. I was worried all the way to Mr. Yancey's ranch. He says come up his way sometime. Go hunting. Like the old days, he says."

"So good to see you, Billy. All of you. There's so much I need to ask you." He looked at Tap. "Maria wouldn't tell me. How did you become Wagner's posse?"

Tap replied, "You'd better ask Bonnie, it was her idea." He exchanged glances with Bonnie. His gaze lingered fondly on her.

"The morning that Wagner rode, the day you met him at the wells, we rode with him. It was still dark when we left the front of the Mountain View and cold. We were bundled to our ears and had our faces covered with bandanas. And something else. We were all riding bays. That's what the Mountain View gang rode after you took Barnes and Olsen away. Wagner came down the back stairs with a bottle in his hand. He hadn't the slightest idea anything was amiss."

"Where was the Mountain View gang?"

"That's where Bonnie's idea comes in," added Trundle. "We were gathered at my place when she dropped the idea on us."

Bonnie smiled at the recognition. "It was pretty simple. Divide and conquer. Pat had ridden in from the ranch, and we got Mr. Gunnison to join us. Beat up as he was, Garvey was there too. We pulled an ore wagon up close to the back of the Mountain View. Inside the saloon, Sonny had the beer flowing freely. When the right people came weaving out to use the outhouse, Pat threw a loop over them. We took their guns and one by one we gagged them, tied them up, and threw 'em in the ore wagon."

Trundle added, "We got all of them but Pelham. We had to let him go. Otherwise, Wagner would have noticed. Soon as we had the men we wanted, Holmes headed off for Silvercrown with them."

Reuben was grinning at Bonnie. "Couldn't have been slicker, Bonnie. How'd you like it if I recommended you for the marshal's job?"

"Not for me, Reuben. We want you. The town wants you. Besides, half that idea came from Maria. You might say we hatched it up together."

"Pelham, what about Pelham?" Reuben wanted to know.

Tap answered, "Garvey arrested him for the jail break and for the murder of Simpson. Beacher's been helping us run watches, and it was Gunnison who wangled the use of the ore wagon.

"As to Wagner, he's gone to Boot Hill. There's some reward money coming. You get half, and the town gets half. The town fathers will use theirs to hire Garvey as full-time deputy."

"They couldn't have found a better man," said Reuben.

"You gonna stay our marshal?" It was Billy asking.

Reuben smiled and took Maria's hand in his. "We will give it a few days more, then we'll decide.

"Soon as I get a little better, I'm goin to plant some late garden. Settle in. The way things are lookin', I won't have to be the law all by myself around here." It got awful quiet. Reuben looked around. Nobody was smiling. Of a sudden, he caught on. "Well, I thought I was working alone. Turns out . . ."

Maria took over then. "Mustn't wear out our patient," she said, herding everyone out of the room.

She stopped at the door, came back and arranged his pillow, bent over, kissed his forehead. He put an arm around her and pulled her close.

Maria thought she caught a worried look on his face. "Are you all right, Reuben? Did we tire you?"

"I'm all right. Just a concern. Could you have Bonnie come back in for a minute?"

Bonnie was there in a moment, closing the door carefully and coming to his bedside. "You had a question, Reuben?"

"Yes, you've been here most of the time, haven't you?"

"I've been back the last three days. I went to Yancey's for Billy."

"And I'm glad you're back, both of ya. But I, ah . . . I need to know, while I've been here recovering, have I talked in my sleep?" He was quiet for a while, and then he asked, "What was I saying?"

She was laughing and vastly pleased about something. There was another pause, and then he asked, "Did I call for anyone?"

"Yes, you called for a woman. No matter who came in the room, you asked for her. Always the same woman."

Concern written all over his pale face, he asked, "Who did I call for?"

He looked so sorrowful that she laughed again. "You can relax, Reuben. You called for Maria, always for Maria."

He broke into a huge smile. "Can you find my pants for me and a shirt?"

A few minutes later, he was sitting at his favorite table overlooking Main Street. Maria came in from the kitchen, a white apron over her red dress. "You are well enough to sit out here, *Jefe*?"

"Yes, thanks to you." He reached for her hand, kissed it. With his other hand, he dug into his britches, found a silver dollar, and plunked it on the table. "Maria, love, bring me beer and steak until this is all gone.

"And salsa. Salsa too."

Edwards Brothers, Inc.
Thorofare, NJ USA
March 6, 2012